Cyr Myrddin

The Coming of Age of Merlin

By

Michael de Angelo

Gododdin Publishing
San Francisco ~ London

First Printing 1979
Second Printing 2009

First Paperback Edition

For the courage of the children…

Tyr Myrddin

The Coming of Age of Merlin

Father, I am alone in an alone land.

I have challenged the gates of Time. I have left your side to tell them. Forgive me, Cyr Myrddin, but it is our place to come here, and by my faith, You will join me. You roamed the twilight forest long, before coming to that dreaded sleep of centuries, when You were laid down in the Enchanted Cave that is the darkness of their minds.

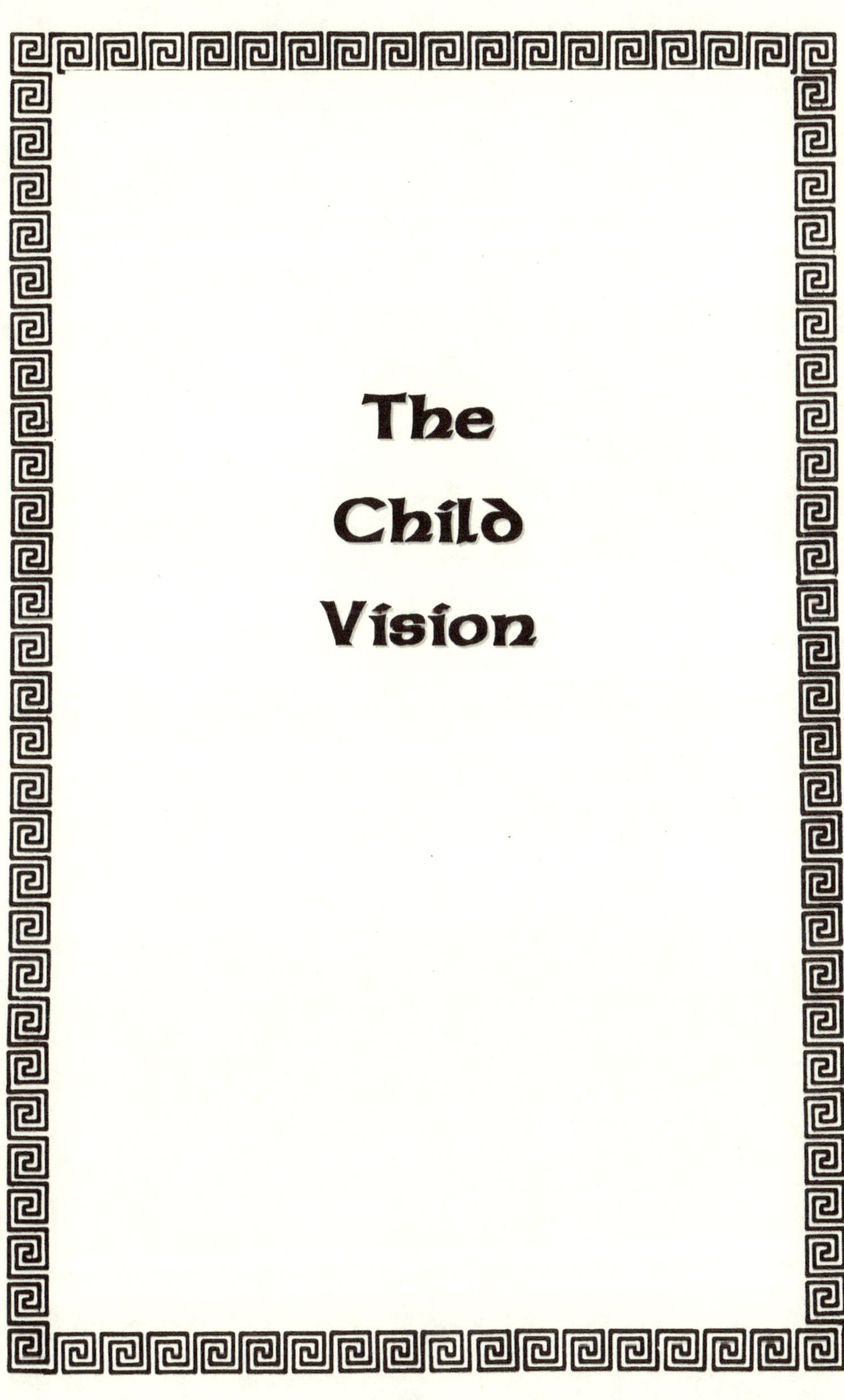

The Child Vision

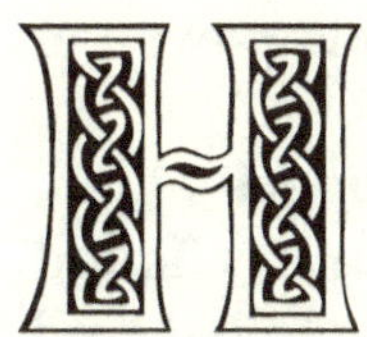

ow he loved, when he was only seven, to listen to the stories and legends told close to the hearth in the hours after the falling sun. Since mid-afternoon he had been waiting anxiously, and now at last came the muffled knocks of trotting hooves, bringing to the door three men, an old woman, and two small children, brother and sister. All entering together, they nodded their greetings and gathered close to the stone fireplace. His mother stooped low to the fire, then carried a flame on a small branch to the wicks of seven candles, whose warm glow seemed to hold not memory of day, but the captured history of night unbroken.

Candle by candle the fire's flame reached outward, in giving itself became two, then three, then four; it stepped upward to the rows of rough hewn crossbeams overhead, groping to fill the shadowy textures on the walls of gray stone block. It hurled long shadows into the lingering darkness, and grew until the yellow aura of a room within a room was all around.

This was his room of dreams, at whose boundary of dimming light he had so often sat huddled in his blanket of brown wool, with his arms wrapped round his legs for warmth, and his chin resting on his knees. For so many nights he had listened through the hours as voice after voice brought alive legendary battles, noble families and courageous warriors, until he could almost hear the ground shaking with the galloping charges of armor-laden horses, and the air filling with the ringing and clashing of swords and shields, while dukes and kings spoke quickly in councils of war.

There were tales of Macsen Wledig, of Pryderi and Manawydan, of Aranrhod and Lleu. He heard of the horse of Rhiannon, that mortal steed could not approach, and of the wondrous Cauldron of Rebirth, that could

restore the life of a dead warrior, save for his power of speech.

Yet for all his love of these tales, this night he felt alone, and the stories could not hold him. Cold drafts found their way through his blanket leaving him chilled and shivering on the dampness of the stone floor. But he felt he must not leave his dark corner to draw closer to the warmth of the fire and the gathering; he only pulled his knees closer to his chest, and wrapped the blanket more tightly around himself. Across the room he could see only the backs of large dark bodies huddled close together near the flames, and the profiles of unfamiliar faces. The flickering of the fire became distant, and the voices grew muffled as though coming from another room. To his mind came instead two very special stories.

It seemed he had always known these stories; their telling warmed him inside like milk poured from the fire's cauldron. One was the tale of a warrior who carried neither sword nor spear, but walked with faith alone onto the battlefield; the other was of a maiden who appeared to a child beside a mountain spring, to bestow upon the waters the power of healing…

Earlier the sun had left the sky in a cascade of amethyst over pale blue; now the nearly full moon illuminated the huge gray clouds piling on the horizon.

Through the arched stone window of his room, an oval of burnished bronze light grew distinct in the coming darkness. It moved slowly over the floor, finally coming to cover a straw mat that lay below the window ledge.

Outside, it was just dark enough to see the few bright stars of the night heavens. Pine boughs were swishing in the quiet.

He awoke in his bed, beneath the warmth of a down quilt. His mother sat beside him stroking his hair, her

face half shadow, half lit in moonlight. She whispered something he did not hear, kissed his forehead, and left. He could not fall back into sleep, but instead grew more awake. He crawled out from under his covers to sit closer to the window, and watch the sky fill with stars, until finally he found himself kneeling on the straw mat, his arms folded on the window ledge.

Minutes passed, left with the wind, poured from the moon, grew cold on the stone against his arms, appeared one by one with the tars, collected breath after breath until the sky was black and brilliant, and he wandered again on the threshold of sleep.

As his head fell into his arms, he imagined himself to be looking upward still into the night sky, watching a ring of golden gray clouds loft upward as their center remained a darkness of ever increasing depth. A music came to his ears that was not music, a harmony without time or tones, like the sound he heard in snow touching ground.

The darkness opened in a shower of blue radiance, and in the stillness becoming more still, he could see men and women looking down upon him from a circular balcony of clouds. Their faces were drawn in textures of fine spun light, with gentleness on the faces of the men, and strength on the faces of the women. Neither young nor old, they all held themselves in noble grace, in ancient ancestral grace.

Their eyes were upon him. A voice came softly, not to his ears, but to a place deep within; he did not know what was said, but he felt a presence enter him...the damp chill of the window ledge finally touched his bones, and he began to stir. The memory of the dream came to him, and he lifted his head to look up into the clouds.

His eyes met theirs – his breath stilled in the ingoing, holding the vision's glow, the faces, the silence. He

touched his own face with his hands, turned his head to look for the familiar shapes of his bedroom. He looked upward again. The wind had begun to move in the sky; the opening in the clouds was closing. He laid his face down on the bed and wept, because he did not understand, and because he did.

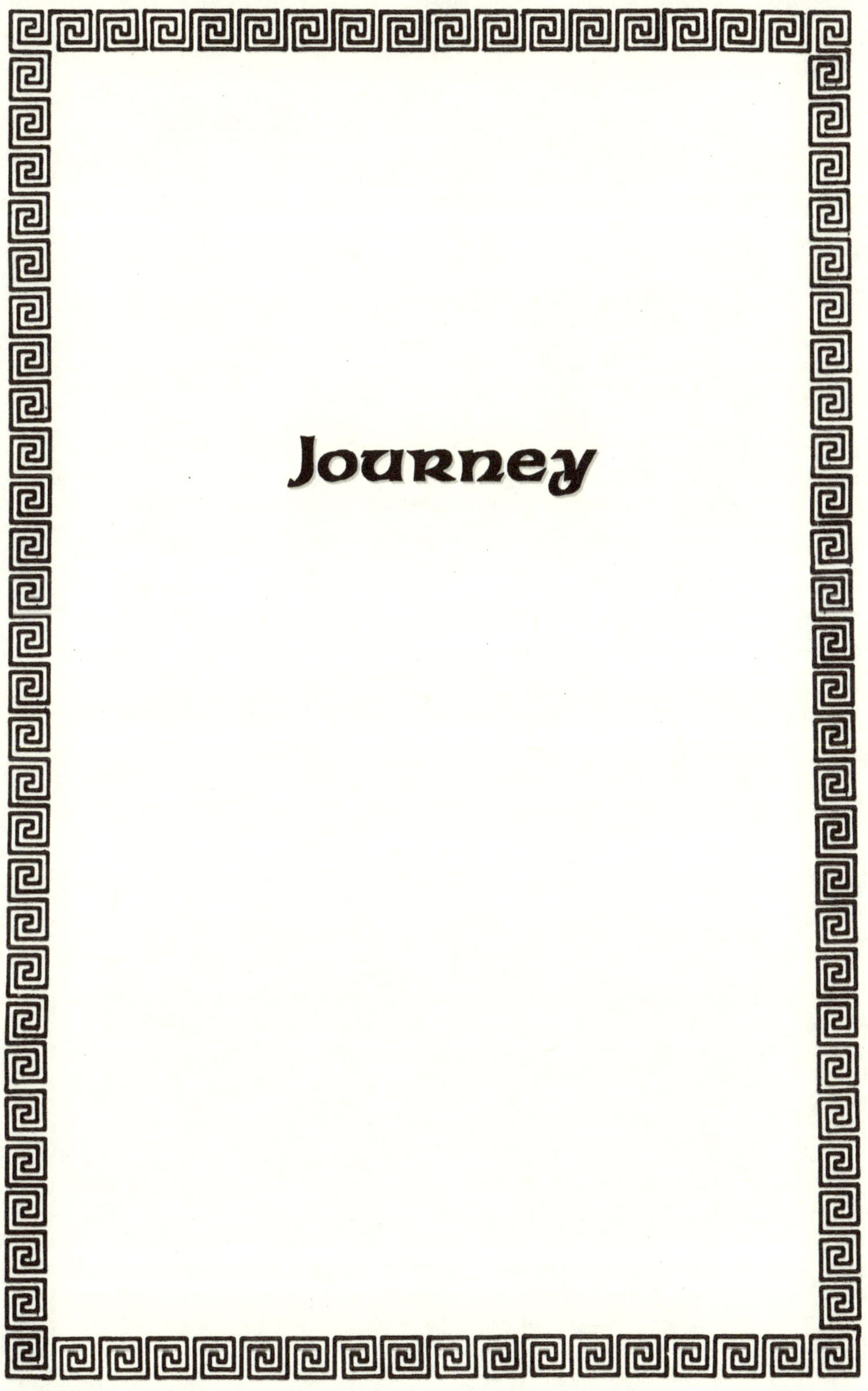

Journey

Some time after the half moon had dropped below the silhouetted elms, when the moon-shadows were gone, and the signs of dawn still lay invisible over the land, Merlin found himself standing in the doorway of his home of seventeen years. As the night's raw wind slid over the back of his neck and hands, he watched the now low flames of the hearth draw the lines of his mother's face. The light shone softly on one side, glimmering on fine but full lips, reflecting on a delicately chiseled nose. Her cheekbones were high, her eyebrows two thin arches on a smooth forehead, and the black of her long hair cast curving shadows over her neck and shoulders. Dark brown eyes, looking outward to him from deep wells, held him incapable of words.

For a moment he looked down, taking her slender fingers in his upturned palms. Then he lifted his eyes to meet hers, and spoke with her in silent gaze. He explained, and she pleaded. She questioned, and he begged for understanding. He demanded, but she did not respond. He gave up hope of having her understand, now waiting only for her blessing. The sadness grew into tears in her eyes, and she nodded once, slowly, because she knew now he would be going, and she would have him go with her love. Tears tried to come to his eyes too, but he held them back. This was not what he had wanted, but it had to be enough.

He let her hands down to her sides, and then turned halfway toward the lighted edge of morning on the eastern hills. He nodded his goodbye, seeing for the last time the smoldering hearth, blankets still lying near the red embers, an iron kettle in the ashes.

He set out. Behind him, the heavy door closed with a thud; the sound ran down the path into the mist. He followed it, leaving the hollow where the house stood in a

small clearing. On the first rise of the trail, he looked back one more time, to see the stone corners holding an edge against the enveloping fog.

Ahead of him the trees closed into a low canopy. The cool grayness of dawn had brought with it a sharp drizzle that pelted his head and shoulders, and stung the backs of his hands. He hastened on. When he entered into the trees, the wind changed, and the branches began to dance, churning the air into the colors of their leaves.

He followed the turns and twists of the trail deeper into the darkness of the forest, where the light filtering through the branches grew less and less. There was some power here in the oaks that towered above him; their massive silence now left his singing as no more than the stirring of wind in an empty vessel. All around him, rain-pools lay in the grasp of gnarled roots, and overhead, branches reached upward in a tangling of hundreds of arms. He kept his eyes to the trail, and quickened his stride.

The trail widened into a narrow rutted road, a rope holding human islands from drifting apart in the green undulating seas. He walked on, through groves possessing shapes and sounds of their own creation, and veins of green pulsing.

He traveled through the dimness of day, as the miles grew behind him. When the few patches of sky finally began to darken and the forest air grew murky, he wondered why he was traveling alone, why he had let nightfall approach so near, to find him still on the road without shelter or thought of defense. Morning had seemed no more than a passing dream, and afternoon a waiting for darkness.

Where was he now? The pillars of dead trees were around him, fallen branches scattered like bones in the dim moonlight. Through the fading light of day, his

eyes caught a reflection in the branches, what seemed to be the form of an uplifted sword.

The rain must have stopped. The splattering of water drops on leaves sounded eerie now, as they dropped down branch to branch. He pulled his cloak more tightly around himself, and his thoughts raced homeward. His mother had given him a new cloak for his journey, along with some barley cakes and mead. He smiled, as for a moment the memory warmed him, but he knew he could not be comforted. The cloak could not withhold cold that had come to dwell in his bones, nor barley cakes feed the hunger that had grown in his mind. Mead could not sweeten the hollowness in his chest and throat.

Something stirred inside him, something old, something that had come many times before. He tried to see into the darkness, but the harder he looked, the darker it became, until the darkness rushed back at him like an enveloping shroud. It was some gnawing restlessness that had found its way into him without his ever knowing.

He looked down to the road, and heard a low groaning voice. `Come with me, friend. I know what it is you seek. Come deeply, come more deeply, for my darkness will soothe all sorrow.'

But he knew the road's cleverness. He stroked the leather grip of the finely wrought iron dagger at his side. He was clever, too. He would walk on until his weariness laid him down. He would rush on to the night's peace, to the silence that would still his thoughts in deepest sleep. He would travel more swiftly than his memories could follow.

The day ended. The dull yellow of the sun mixed with the gray of the clouds.

The air, still churning from its rainy upheaval, filled with the dampness of the ground and trees. He would

have to find somewhere to lay his blanket, somewhere he would not be discovered, where he would know if anyone was to approach.

The trail brought him to a rocky hillside that held only a few trees. Halfway up, he saw a small plateau of rock surrounded by scraggly shrubs. Nearby, a foot-wide stream had cut a line of white stone through sweeps of grass and scattered brown leaves. With the last slow steps of his day, he struggled up the hill. When he reached the outcropping, he let himself fall onto his hands and knees, and began to pull deep breaths into his stomach. The air hissed in his throat, filling the quiet. The stream trickled and poured down into tiny pools.

He crawled over to it, holding a hand against its gentle flowing. It was cool and soothing. He leaned forward on all fours, with his palms against the moist ground to either side. Lowering his mouth to the running water, he sucked it deep into his throat, and drank again and again. Above him now the stars sat in a black sky, a thousand bright stars, and a myriad more faintly glowing. He craned his neck back to look upward into the heavens.

For the first time he saw, and understood, that it was night, not day, that was always around him.

He stood up to look over the ground. The fog had cleared, and now he could see down through the valley where it opened into the bay.

For a moment he watched the dull glow of moonlight on the water as it shifted slowly wave to wave. Then he turned his eyes back to the ground. He found the level place for which he was looking, and squatted down to brush the stones away with the edge of his hand, and pull the larger ones out. He unrolled his two blankets, lay on his back on top of one, and pulled the other one between himself and the sky.

The sky grew blacker, the stars brighter. From a few scattered landmarks he guessed that he had come over eighteen miles from the south since morning. Tomorrow he would be traveling beyond the roads he knew.

The mud was hard underneath him now; its small ridges pressed into his back. His breath fell back on his face in a cool gray vapor. The ground reached upward in its chilling wetness to take hold of his back and legs, until he could feel the day's sweat growing cold on his body. He turned on his side, curling his arms and legs tightly against himself. He fell toward a sleep that was shallow enough to be disturbed by the occasional prowling of a small animal, but at last the blankets began to hold some warmth, and the world fell far away...

In a cavern deep in the earth a river was flowing. It glowed in green and brown phosphorescence, moving in slow, slow currents. Above, through a deep crevice, a light poured down onto the brown rocks in a yellow haze.

There were the shapes of six or seven men sitting on the cavern floor, huddled together near the river light. Playing some sort of game, they never spoke, or turned their heads from the circle.

All was silent, no sound for years. . . the sound of the river's flowing, silent, because ever present. They had been born here, just as they were sitting, ages ago. Around them, skeleton pieces lay scattered in a whitish glow. He was one of the men, but now he stood up, moved away from the circle. He stood watching the slow turning of the river, the paleness on the faces of his companions, and the place where the river flowed on beneath a low ceiling of rock.

When he awoke, the sky was dark; he wondered if the pale light was the dawn, or the moon that had come up

after he had gone to sleep. The night was still, no sounds of waking yet.

He did not feel well rested; his sleep had been filled with a strange uneasiness.

How much longer was it until dawn?

He thought he would not be able to sleep again. He closed his eyes for a few minutes, hoping a faint glimmer of morning light might be there when he opened them again.

Stretching his body, he felt the stiffness in his limbs, and the soreness where his hips and shoulders had rested against the hard ground.

He waited, trying to rest. A single bird called out. Another answered. Not much longer now, he thought.

For a long time there were no sounds again. He yawned, several deep yawns.

The birds started calling again. More joined in. A large black bird flew low over him. Morning was coming so slowly he could hardly see the color of the sky growing into ever lighter shades of gray. On the horizon, thick gray clouds held the sunlight.

He got up, rolled his blankets loosely, and began to walk stiffly down the road. His clothes were damp with sweat and rubbed on his skin. He stamped his feet on the ground, and rubbed his hands together to warm them from their dull chill.

He had expected the walking to become easier after the first few miles, but it grew more difficult. Gradually, his steps became sluggish and plodding, and his arms hung down limply at his sides. His body swayed back and forth as he walked.

What he had hoped to escape, the night had brought closer to him.

From somewhere, something was calling him. His pace had slowed into an occasional forward stumbling, until finally he stopped.

Must I know something? Must I know – nothing? Whether I truly know it or not, whether it is real or not, must I know? Knowing is the thread by which I call myself alive. Or is it? Because then I have been dead for a very long time. And nothing is alive I do not know. Nothing seems alive. Who is with me? Who lends me my life in their eyes? Forest, where do you lead me? You grant a place to trees and birds, but I fear you cannot do as much for me. I must find my own way through your groves – I cannot wait. How can I go on without knowing my beginning?

Now his eyes saw what lay before him, a pile of black and withered leaves, but no longer leaves. Decay had made them into only a transparent web of veins. A wind stirred on the forest floor. The leaves crumbled, dispersing into tiny threads that vanished in the dark air.

He heard the sound of his breath in and out his mouth, and could feel the blood pulsing in his temples, in his throat and eyes.

Beyond this valley, greater valleys? Ahead, a point of dissolution, a point of separation, a point of nothingness? Our lives we seem to experience in deepest sleep, with perhaps a few moments of awakening, when we know that we are alive, born of the elements to breathe and see and feel. And beyond the threshold of death, a neglected realm. Sleep, sleep, die, never to awaken to the miracle of our own livingness. Miracle! Miracle! If only the word were enough...but when on the swift passage to the end there comes that unfortunate glimpse of life, what remains but to rage against the messenger. Sleep not, never lived! Die not, never lived! I want to see. I want to awaken to all the world. I want to touch, and be touched. I want to suffer...the trees suffer in winter, burned by the cold touch of the frost… but they behold its crystal vision, its white thousand-faced beauty. I want to look down on the earth from high above, knowing the air

with the birds. I want...why does only my death seem real?

From somewhere his mother's voice came to him, and he could almost feel her presence as she asked in a gentle voice, 'My son, why have you left me alone?'

Within himself, he spoke back to her. `No, mother, it is I that am alone. My love is not what you would imagine. It is not what you would want from me, or could even understand. Because if there is anything in life, anything that makes it more than some dreaming journey from womb to grave, I want to find it. I know there is nothing else for me, there could never be. My life means nothing without it. I have no fear of dying, and I sense what I seek may lie beyond the threshold of that great darkness. So that is where I will go; I can ask no one to go with me. I will leave no door unopened, no room unentered. This is my power: I am not afraid.'

His mother grew distant; he shouted after her, and when his shouting had stopped, he found himself in a room. Its walls were covered in rich tapestries of mountains, lakes, and villages – no windows to intrude upon the weaving of their fine colors. The room was warm, heated by fires in many hearths, and lighted with lamps of scented oil. Strewn everywhere were the remains of years of feasting. In the center, raised on a platform, the master of the house lay on thick embroidered cushions, dying. His eyes and mouth lay nearly hidden in layers of fat, as he spoke in proud tones to the friends and servants gathered around him.

`My life has been one of peace, scholarly learning, and charity to the unwashed. God has granted me fulfillment within these very walls. Now I go content to my final rest.'

He waved an arm, and four servants brought forth his funeral bier. They placed it beside him, and helped him

to roll over onto it, pulling his fat arms, pushing against the great haunches.

Before he could settle again, Merlin stepped forward. 'Do you not fear to go outside, where you have never been?' he asked.

The activity in the room ceased. All eyes turned to glare at him.

The master looked angrily at him, but then, after a moment's reflection, spoke in a soft luring voice. 'Come, friend, and look at these.' He pointed to a wall covered with shelves of beautiful leather-bound manuscripts, with carefully engraved covers. He waited until all in the room had nodded and smiled knowingly, and then continued, 'In these one might learn of all the world, and the mysteries of the heavens. I have read them sincc I was a child. Could one really ask for more?'

'You might ask to see,' Merlin responded sternly.

'But this is the way God has given me to see.'

'Liar!' Merlin raised his voice in accusation. 'You disguise your worship. Your gods are of your own making!'

The master's face became twisted with fright, and grew pale as he struggled to stammer his last words. 'But you also worship!'

Merlin grew outraged and began to shout. 'Worship? Here is my worship – to be crushed by others' suffering as well as my own, to boil in the blood of my own madness until I cry the cry of death, to be ever and ever falling from all sight. This, and this alone, is the, altar of the beginning.'

As he spoke, the master's face grew more and more pale. The flesh began to dry up, began to fall from his rotting white cheekbones. But in his still opened eyes, a window into another room was growing. Merlin looked through it to see his mother lifting her tunic from her soft white breast, where a child was crying for suck . . .

Journey

The stillness was around, was around the night. Without his knowing, the day had passed. Now the cool of twilight, with its red and gold sky, brought him again to the forest. A halo shimmered softly yellow around a half moon that hung low over the wooded hills. Grains of darkness began to gather, drifted like snow, settled into hollows, fell on branches.

He had left the forest trail some miles back, hoping to avoid danger. Now the smaller trail that he had been following lost itself in a scattering of rocks and bushes. He stopped. He sought direction, looking through the trees and shadows, and the amber air. Letting his breath out, he listened. He could hear only the sound of leaves stirring in the evening wind.

Suddenly, to his left, he heard a distinct rustling. Stilling his breath, he turned slowly and silently toward the sound. It seemed to be coming from a small hollow about a stone's throw away. The sound repeated, a thrusting in the leaves, again, again. He put his right hand over the hilt of his dagger, crouching his body low, listening. For a moment it was silent; then it came, again, again. He summoned his strength and his courage, waiting without breath or movement. His thoughts began to race. `I will have to kill. That is my only defense...in these woods, the only trust is the dead man's.'

The sound came louder; he could not keep his breath from quickening. `If I run now, they will only find me more quickly. Maybe they have not yet seen me.' He drew his knife, and held it in the air before him. He listened harder. No, the sound was not getting louder, it was only that he was straining more and more to hear. He let out a long breath. He realized now the sound had not moved closer at all, but at each time had come from the same place in the forest. Perhaps there was no danger

after all. Still holding the moonlit blade before him, he began to approach the sound.

He walked slowly over a small mound of earth, towards the hollow, passing through the last thicket of trees. As he strained his eyes to see through the dark air, the sound became a barely visible shape. He moved closer. There, amidst a cluster of thick black roots, lay a brown and white doe.

On her white patches of fur the moonlight was shining. He watched silently as she lifted her head up over her shoulder, straining to pull her legs underneath her. But her head fell back to the ground, her rear leg kicking against the soil as she tried over and over. Then he saw it.

Sunk deep in her fur covered flesh, just behind the small left foreleg, the broken end of a coarse arrow shaft protruded. A dark stain ran from it over her underbelly. He ran his fingers through it; the blood was warm and red and thick.

He stood over her, watching, wondering how far she had come since she had taken the arrow. From observing its depth and place in her flesh it seemed almost miraculous that she had eluded her hunter. Still, it was an ill fate, he thought, since does are rarely hunted in this season...yet every creature must struggle for – the doe's gaze struck him as a clear voice speaking his name. Come closer, friend, it seemed to say.

He approached, kneeling down beside her, captured by the depths of her brown eyes. For a moment, the crossing rhythms of their breathing was the only sound in the night air. Broken orange moonlight diffused in a tinted haze over her body. Merlin drew his shortsword from its scabbard.

The harsh cry of a raven broke the silence. He had never killed before, but it would be a kindness now, to release this creature from its suffering. He raised his

sword for the stroke, over the base of the small neck. He took one short breath, turning his eyes down slightly. The moon emerged in its full brightness from behind misty clouds, casting man and animal in copper tableau – he gasped, lowering his arm.

It could not be, he thought. It was too late. He shuddered, words passing from his lips, without his knowing. "My God!"

The doe's belly was swollen with fawn.

The doe strained her head upward to look into his eyes, and this time he understood. What could he do? There was no time. He must think...he was afraid to cut into her belly while she was still alive; he could not kill her. He could not wait until she died, or the fawn would die too. But her exertion had most likely already begun the labor. He closed his eyes for a long moment, searching for his strength, trying to recall from the birthing of his own foal something that might help him now.

There was only one way. He pulled off his cloak and bundled it under her hindquarters. The night chill hit his skin as he kneeled down behind her in a pool of blood and water.

The birth canal had begun to open. He pulled out his dagger, found its sharpest edge, and with one swift draw made a cut through the muscles of the opening. There was little blood. Covering the knife's point with his forefinger, he probed upward into the canal, searching for the membrane of the sack. But with his hand around the knife blade, the opening was too small. He pushed his hand up alone, up to the wrist. When his fingertips felt the thin tissue, he dug into it with his fingernails until it tore. The waters gushed in a warm stream over his hand, pouring into a pool at his knees.

He knew he would have to work quickly now. If the mother was dying, any contractions would soon diminish,

causing the birth canal to close, trapping the infant within.

He pushed one arm up into the warm silken flesh. He was breathing heavily now, and the taste of sweat was on his lips. His hand searched for the tiny head and shoulders. The head was lying slightly to the side of the forelegs; he moved it to rest directly upon them. Above in the tress, the wind danced, and a few birds called, the soft hooting of an owl, and the hoarse grates of a night-jar.

Digging his knees against the ground, he struggled to push his hand in deeper. He felt the contractions against his forearm growing weaker. The doe was very still now, and he feared she would no longer be helping him with the birth. He curled over on his side, bracing his knees against the white hindquarters. Inside her womb, he spread his fingers into a shallow bowl, and pulled gently and steadily, forming a cradle with his forearm to protect the fragile head and neck. Forcing his other hand up into the opening, he took hold of the forelegs. The head began to slowly emerge. He drew in a deep breath, and the rest of the body followed in one swift motion. He held in his arms a cream colored fawn with wet fur and closed eyes.

He wiped the mucus from its mouth with his fingers. Covering its mouth with his own, he breathed gently into its lungs. As the tiny chest rose and fell with each breath, he waited, and watched for some response. He rubbed its spine up and down several times with his palm. At last it gasped, and drew its first breath. Its back arched outward, and the lids on two brown almond eyes flickered and opened.

He laid it down on the grass, taking the umbilical cord in his hand to feel its pulse. He cut two thin strips of wool from his blanket, tied one on the cord near the mother, and the other near the belly of the fawn. With his knife he cut through the cord.

For a few moments the fawn lay perfectly still in the moonlight, breathing the night air as the wind, growing more brisk, stroked its fur. Then, with a shake of its head, it pushed itself up onto its thin forelegs, and with another push, up onto its hind legs. It walked to the doe in a few short wobbling steps, and began to explore her body with its nose. She did not lift her head, or open her closed eyes. The fawn laid down on the soil close to her underbelly, to nestle in her fading warmth.

Merlin lifted the fawn gently into the cradle of his arms, wrapping it in a blanket. He looked down to where the doe lay, wondering if she knew that she had given birth, but was unable to tell whether she was still breathing. He felt the heat of the fawn's body against his chest, and heard its shallow breathing. He ran his fingers over the flopping ears and tiny hooves, and looked once more into its brown eyes before pulling the blanket closed.

It returned his gaze, and then snuggled up to the bare skin of his neck. The doe was silent.

He began to walk, knowing he would walk through the night. Still, dreams would come. The hours passed. Enchanted by the unchanging rhythm of his own steps, he moved through the branches overhead into the starlit sky. Here was a night of stars, holding what secrets only the brave might know. Here was a night of black seas, where crystal ships voyaged laden with wonders of all the heavens. The Messenger approached; the Presence surrounded him.

He traveled on and on in the endless sky, through the hours and the miles. His feet splashed through small streams. The trees cried out, crying his loneliness, his sadness, his exhaustion.

He ran with the life in his arms, until dawn came to him, bathing him in its soft warmth. The smell of damp moss and rotting leaves rose from the forest bed.

Journey

The sun appeared, a layered ribbon of orange and gray on a hill horizon barely visible through the trees. The branches overhead became a fine stiff lace.

What more could he have done? The fawn, still and silent in his arms, had followed its mother into the other world, seeking still another womb. Now he heard each gust of wind as a death knell for a thousand crimson gold leaves, descending in swirls to ground and water, settling amidst seedlings and fallen trees. A single leaf landed on the pouring water of a stream, turned over and over in a momentary backwater, rushed on. Stepping softly through the crops of scarlet toadstools growing up from the russet cloth of the forest floor, the sycamore keys whirled downward, onto slippery piles of red and yellow and brown leaves; ferns turned in the wind, their webs of dew reflecting glimmers of morning light. The sparrows were hunting.

He hoped somewhere there would be a place. He could brush the wet leaves away, and scrape a hollow in the soft brown soil.

Stopping Place

he snow came falling, gentle and sparse all around him, minute by minute filling the air with its downward swirling. Snowflakes descended as patches of downy cloth, knit together as white shadows on the branches. He held a hand out, and watched as four or five completed a tiny blanket, before the heat of his skin began to melt them.

He curled up his fingers to form a hollow in his palm clear water.

He let the water run off his hand, then lifted his gaze to look deeply into the falling snow, until only streaming veils of white surrounded him, and it seemed he was rising ever upward within them. For a few moments, the snowfall made his world complete, and he was uplifted. The wind stopped. The snow fell straight down.

The faun's death, its momentary life, lingered in him, growing within him. He wanted to cry out in protest, but he knew there would be no one to hear him, no one to listen to that other certain fear, a fear that he knew was not his alone.

But now he could only listen to the soft padding of his feet through the snow, as he placed one foot before the other, as though steadying his spirit.

The days had passed; he was walking the high ridges now. At times, in places where trees could not hold the rocky slopes, he could look down into the valleys, and see the lines of hills stacked one behind another on the horizon.

He had nowhere to go, and so walked slowly. Time and destination were of no concern. But he listened, as he needed with all his heart to listen.

He did not know now why he had left home, or whether there was yet another home drawing him on. He only knew he could not return. Blessing the wind, he asked it to carry him to his fate.

Stopping Place

A few leaves tumbled end over end across his path. He looked up from his feet shuffling through the leaves and twigs, and caught for a moment a glimpse of three high peaks as they appeared through the shifting clouds.

The road was long; he grew hungry and cold. He had eaten the last of his barley cakes some days back thinking he could manage a few days without food, but now he regretted his decision. The mead too was gone. As he walked, he looked for water. He found some dribbling down a rock face to the side of the trail. He put his mouth to the rock, letting the cool and clear water run over his lips and chin as he drank. Then he filled his goatskin pouch.

The water strengthened him, but he knew he would have to eat if he were to stay warm. He became angry with himself as he thought how he had packed in such haste; if he had thought to bring along some kind of rope, he could have used it now to set some snares. But then he was not sure he could remember how to do it, and trying to remember where he had placed them might prove difficult in an unfamiliar wood.

So instead, when he came to the next stream, he gathered a pile of smooth round stones, wrapping them in a bundle in one of his blankets. He picked up a few more, and went in search of unwary squirrels. After laboring for some time under the weight of the stones, he decided they were too heavy, and emptied half of them out.

Finally he spotted one. He put down his bundle to get a good throw, but the rocks clattered, and the emptiness in his stomach ached as the squirrel went scampering high into the branches. Exasperated, he threw his rock at it just the same. It shot through the branches, and began to fall back again, bouncing down so that he could not tell where it would fall; he covered his head with his arms

and ran out from under the tree as the rock shot down barely missing him. He would have to spot the squirrel farther away.

He walked the trail again; many hours went by before he had another chance. Then at last he saw another. Quietly removing his load, he began to approach, lifting his arm for the throw. Stepping lightly, not too close, but close enough to – ugh! The stone sailed wide, and another squirrel escaped safely into the branches, chattering down its annoyance.

He began to realize how cold he was. His fingers and ears were nipped, almost numb. His whole body was growing cold and weak. His feet, too, felt stiff. His resolve to live alone in the wilds was quickly fading. This adventure could be taken up some other time, but now he was cold, and to freeze to death would accomplish nothing. He had to leave the mountain; he had to find a friendly village where he might find good food, and a warm bed, and hear human voices once again.

He pressed forward in haste, following the trail over great humps of stone thrown upward by the earth. As he came around the final crest of rock, the vista opened downward. He could see the valley far below, a deep furrow cut between two steep mountains. His eyes followed the rock slopes down to the green pastures, down through fields of burnt orange fern. At the bottom lay a lake, like a bowl of water gathered in the hollow of the mounds. The water glimmered with the orange light of a sun beginning to fall below the hills. Above him, the clouds and mists were moving in to cover the ridge tops from which he had descended. Across the valley, a small stream plunged in a rock furrow down the hillside, filling the air all around with white spray before joining the silent lake below. This valley, he felt, held something for him, something safe and warm, and peace giving. It

would be a good place to find comfort after so many weeks alone.

A rain began to fall. It pressed his hair down cold and wet on his forehead, and soaked through his clothes. But it no longer mattered. Now that he had chosen to leave his communion with the wilds, images of home life returned to him, images of warm hands, and caring voices, trustful eyes, flaming hearths, and hot gruel in his belly. Released from his own chosen ordeal, he became clear-minded and light-hearted, almost elated. His weariness dissolved; strength returned. His eyes brightened, and he smiled.

The trail down the hillside criss-crossed back and forth as it descended. But now no trail was needed; his eyes searched out a more direct path, and he began to run straight down the hill. The slope was steep and covered with layers of rock chips. At first, balance was difficult, but soon he had moved into a graceful rhythm of leaping. Each step fell hard onto the stones, displacing them as his foot slid downward. When the sliding ended and the stones were once more packed solidly beneath his foot, he leaped off in along stride to land on his other foot. Leap, land, slide, left, right, leap, land, slide, leap, land slide…the sound of the stones, kerick, kerashhh, ke-rick, kerashhh...he grew bolder, taking ever longer leaps outward, landing far below on the hill. His breathing came faster and harder. His feet at last found the pasture; his strides grew still longer. He imagined himself pushing outward toward the sky in long glides, to land on the hill three strides below. Faster and higher he leaped, gliding though the air, gliding. His feet found stepping places faster than his eyes could spot them, dancing over rocks, weaving between shrubs, skirting clumps of grass, floating above the small gullies. As he ran, he began to wail, only to send his voice through the valley, over the

ground and into the sky; he pushed his breath into the great expanse.

He came to the outskirts of the village; he ran through the animal pastures, scattering the sheep bleating, dodging the cows that moved too slowly. Approaching the circular earthworks surrounding the village, left unguarded by day, he ran down into the ditch to climb up the man-made hill on the other side.

His legs felt as though they were about to collapse beneath him, as he saw, upon pushing over the crest, that he was still far from any buildings. He stopped for a moment, letting himself sway with the slight breeze, and watched the golden sun pouring red over the forested hills. His breath burned and rattled harshly in his throat. He began to run again, down onto a trail fenced by woven willow sticks. The straw cones of roofs drew closer until he could see the loose patches of stone and wattle on their sides. He was breathing much too heavily, gasping; his legs, no longer feeling, fell forward one after the other. He could go only a few hundred more steps, wanting to collapse, to wrap his arms and legs tightly around himself, to be warm. His throat burned, raw, painful. Faint now, faint, his eyes unclear; not far to his sides, smudges of human figures were watching him now. Stumbling before a great stone cistern…the sound of pouring water – a well.

He picked himself up from the ground, remaining on his knees. With his elbows, he pulled himself up to the rim of the cistern, where the water ran over in a thin sparkling sheet. He let his face fall forward to the cold water, and drank through pursed lips.

He leaned back to look upward, the sun a fiery half-circle casting long red and orange flames over a gray sky.

Nausea filled his stomach and chest; the ground began to spin; he tried to hold on. He felt himself sliding back onto his knees against the side of the stone, then falling

flat to the ground, his arms without the strength to keep his face from hitting the dirt. Its gritty taste filled his mouth; his hearing faded on stray shouts, and steps coming.

He awoke looking upward into the peak of a straw roof, with the weight of coarse wool blankets over him, and the warmth of a body sitting beside him on the bed. A strong but slender hand held the back of his head, a soft hand, warm and healing. He felt her breath over his face. Outside, a sparrow called.

She, whispered to him. "Friend, friend... "

The sun coming through an open doorway warmed his bed. He opened his eyes, through the window the sky a milky blue.

As she leaned over him, he tried to move his fingers to touch her shoulder, but he could not move his hand. He was still buried too deeply in his body, his will unable to direct his own muscles. She turned her face toward him. A shudder ran through his chest. He tried to speak, straining to open his eyes more widely. He struggled to move his head, his lips, but could not. Yet he knew her. Deeply within him, a memory stirred from some distant time and place. Once he had held her, close, had known her beauty – the memory left his mind, returning to its dwelling place.

Once again he was safe and warm, and perhaps for a while home. He fell back into a rich dream-filled sleep he was not sure he had ever left.

When he finally awoke, he did not know how long he had slept, but it seemed to be early morning. He heard the sound of stone grinding against stone; he raised his head, and through the low doorway, saw a child turning the handle of a stone quern around and around. He laughed softly to himself; this was the first time he had ever seen someone grinding grain.

Outside, the sky was growing into ever lighter shades of

blue. He yawned and curled up under the warm blankets, thinking he would sleep for several hours more.

"Will you take breakfast with us?" It was the voice of a young boy.

"What?" Merlin asked."

"My father says if you feel better we wish you to come to the table."

"Oh." Merlin thought it was very early to be rising – it was still dark.

The boy took his response as sufficient and left.

Merlin dressed and walked out to the main room, not knowing what to expect. Unsure of himself, he stood motionless for a moment before an old woman with brown teeth and sparkling eyes took him by the arm and led him to the table.

"Yes, that's right, that's right. Make yourself at home," she spoke in a matronly soothing tone.

Those gathered at the table offered him, cheerful smiles and encouraging looks. These seemed to be good people, he thought. As he sat down, another woman, middle-aged, ladled steaming barley gruel into his bowl. It seemed he had never smelled anything so good in his whole life. A bowl of small green apples was passed around; he took one of them.

Then everyone nodded their heads for a moment in silent grace, except the young boy, who giggled softly and peered out of the top of his eyes at Merlin. Merlin met his eyes, and smiled.

They took up their spoons and began to eat.

Merlin studied the faces around the table. The old woman's face was deeply wrinkled, but her skin was tough and leathery. Her blue-gray eyes glowed with a simple faith, perhaps born of years of watching life pass before her. She was called Yetta. The face of the other woman was worn, but her skin still held taut on her

bones. Her brown hair, coarse chopped, bleached by the sun, hung down straight to her broad shoulders; her clear brown eyes already looking to the day's work ahead. The little boy's beaming eyes seemed to hold some secret, darker than the smile he usually carried. But whatever brooded within him, he seemed content now to enjoy the hearty taste of the barley. The man's hair and beard was reddish blond in waves. His face, worn by the wind and the sun, seemed contoured in stone, and his calm and discerning eyes looked to the year's harvest.

Merlin turned his gaze to the young woman; his spoon fell into his bowl with a splash. All this time she had been watching him.

Now she laughed, and a mischievous glimmer danced in her crystal blue eyes. Her smile was beautiful to behold….her rose colored lips set against creamy skin and white teeth...shining blond hair tossed over small shoulders, her nose finely sculptured, with high cheekbones and –

"I am Dane." The man looked up from his empty bowl. "What is your name, son?" he asked somewhat sternly.

"I am called Merlin."

"Well, Merlin, God only knows what you are doing roaming around in the hills, where only the wild people dare to go. But if you can be trusted, and have a mind to work, we'll give you some warm clothes, and you can stay in the empty stall. Our ox died last spring. We will talk more when the day's work is done." In so saying, he rose and left the table.

The others, more curious and less strict about their working hours, stayed on to question him.

"Where have you come from now, my son?" Ora, his wife, asked.

"Maridinum, to the south on the sea," Merlin replied.

"It has been a long journey then?"

"Yes, very long," Merlin said.

"From the sea, from the sea," Rudd, the little boy repeated. "Are there pirates?"

"Often enough," Merlin replied.

"Are there sea monsters?" he asked, excited to find a possible source of some new adventure stories.

"I cannot say as I have been looking for them."

"Will you be with us for a while then?" Yetta asked.

"I do not really know," Merlin answered.

"Well, you will be welcome as long as you wish to stay, and I hope you have a strong back." This seemed to conclude the meeting. Everyone left for the day's labors, except for the young woman, who waited until they had all left the room before turning her attention to him.

"I am Branwen," she announced, as though it would be of some importance to him. She smiled with close lips, opening her eyes wide, and cocking her head slightly to one side. Then she looked into his eyes, turned, and left.

"Oh!" Merlin thought to himself. He went back to his sleeping place to look for his cloak. Throwing it over himself, he stepped out into the day through the low doorway. The sudden brightness made him squint. He took a deep breath of the clear morning air, less filled with the smell of dung and straw than his stall had been. He looked over to the eastern hills, where the sun burned reddish gold through the last rising bank of white mist. With the mist clearing, the deep green of the pastures seemed almost to glow. It was truly a blessed valley, and he could almost imagine himself remaining, were it not for the more important work that lay ahead of him.

He jumped back as a dozen sheep swept before him, bleating loudly. An old woman walked behind them, driving them on with a stick. As she passed before him, he saw her large humped nose, and small black eyes. She grinned at him, a large, three-toothed grin, and hobbled by. A small girl followed, carrying a brown chicken in her arms. With her small legs she had to run to keep

up with the old woman's shuffling. He watched them grow distant on the road, the dirt brown fleece of the sheep becoming a dark haze moving over two dirt tracks. He thought the sheep seemed lean.

He guessed that he had been left free to explore the village today. But he was not really interested in the village activities; he had his own thoughts to consider. He looked over the hillside, searching for a quiet place where he might be alone. He began to follow a stream that led out of the village through a few small patches of trees. He was relieved to soon find himself beyond the noise and business of the morning. Continuing for almost two miles along the course of the stream, he came at last to a trail leading up the hillside. He climbed it, over a small ridge. From the top, he could see the path tracing its way back down the other side. Far below, it reached a chasm, spanned by an arched bridge built of stone and mortar. At the bottom of the wide chasm a stream cut its way deeper into the rock, now running nearly two hundred feet below its first ancient course, dropping into ever lower valleys toward the horizon.

He made his way down to the bridge. The sun was still behind him, pouring streams of red over the gray sky, coloring the stones, the trees and the air. As he drew closer he heard the soft roar of the rushing water far below. He sat on the stones, feeling the cool stillness all around.

The bridge was perhaps a hundred years old, or more. How many others, he thought, had sat where he now sat, watching the day begin? And before, how many years of hard labor had made this bridge, how many years of men's lives? Had they watched as the exhausting days had become months? Cutting and hauling blocks, fixing them in mortar...was there no more to life than such simple and consuming tasks?

He sensed his own work was of more importance and

urgency. These simple people could not hear the calling, or assist in giving birth to life not of the body. They did not know the vital moment, or understand that life was but a doorway. For him, there was no rest, only growth, calling to be fulfilled.

The sun grew warm on his back and shoulders. He walked over to the shade of an elm tree and lay down in the grass. As he was about to enter a restful sleep, he heard voices. He looked up to see a group of children climbing down from the ridge, guided by an older child. He was surprised they had been able to climb the hill.

Finally, they reached a clearing of low grass not far from him. He had never really watched children playing before; his own childhood had been friendless, and so he had shared none of the usual activities of that time. He stood to approach them more closely.

There were eleven or twelve of them ranging in ages from maybe five to seven. As he watched their playing, a peacefulness grew inside him. He sat down on the ground again, near a large evergreen tree that opened its branches low over the ground.

The children ran in all directions, laughing and shouting at each other, kicking up the dirt. A small girl was accidentally knocked down, and began to weep. Two boys only slightly older, helped her to stand again, and then put their arms around her until she stopped weeping.

Away in a corner of the field, another boy stood courageously in battle. The wind crept up on him from behind, knocking his hat off with a swift and certain stroke. The boy looked around surprised, and reached down to put his hat back on. Again, the wind charged. Again the hat blew to the ground, even as his hand closed on the air above his head. He retrieved the hat and put it back on his head, pulling the corners securely over his ears, then stood motionless, with a quizzical look on his

face, as though plotting to outwit this new menace. The wind gusted; the hat flew off. Exasperated, he threw his open hand at the invisible tormentor, shouting, "Stop that!"

Merlin watched intently, not noticing the boy who had walked slowly around the tree he sat under, and who now approached him cautiously from behind. But after a time, he felt someone watching him, and turned around. The child continued to step slowly and quietly toward him; when he had approached within a few feet, he stopped, and, leaning back, intertwined his arms with the soft branches of the tree. He seemed afraid, not lifting his eyes from the ground. He swayed his body in the branches, letting them carry his weight. At last he looked up, and their eyes met. Merlin smiled. The child smiled and sat down beside him, with his body touching Merlin's. For a while they sat together without speaking, and Merlin felt his loneliness softening.

The child was the first to break the silence. "Who are you?"

"I, or no one," Merlin replied.

"I or no one?" The child laughed, amused. "Who are you really?"

"Oh, a wayfarer, I suppose."

"But what's your name," he demanded.

"Names are not important . . . but mine is Merlin."

"Then you are Merlin!" he exclaimed excitedly with a tone of insistence.

"Yes, perhaps that is who I am, or what I am." Neither of them spoke for a long time, but they sat there together, the warm afternoon wind blowing between them…

In the main group, the older boy was gathering the children together. Merlin's young friend saw that he had to go. He smiled a missing tooth grin, wrinkling his small freckled nose. Then, with an unsuccessful wink of one of

his green eyes, he jumped up to join the group.

Soon they were all out of sight, and Merlin was alone once again.

For a while he listened to the sound of the stream below, before beginning to climb back up the hill. Soon he was again in the vicinity of the village. He did not approach the huts; instead, he walked to the opposite shore of the lake, and sat down at the water's edge. Across the lake, he could see the reflection of a cone-shaped roof in the water.

There was something he felt about these people, something they seemed to have that he did not. He let his eyes roam over the valley, from the small scrubby patches of orange brown grass at his feet, to the rounded gray blocks of the hills rising up to the low clouds. Sweeps of green pasture ran from shore to hillside, the tall wild grasses above. On the slopes, small trees nestled in the flatter hollows, amidst fields of dark burnt orange ferns. Still higher, the patchwork gray cliffs, cut and crossed with small ledges, shelves of clustered green, lone spots of white, the sheep grazing high today. Patches of bright blue within fleecy white clouds, on the horizon, black and gray clouds, the driving wind high above.

This valley seemed to him a stopping place, an uncertain rest. He could no longer have a home; this was a longing he sensed he would never fulfill.

The sun was falling low in the sky, casting a glint of red on the water. The wind grew stronger, whipping inches of white waves against the shore of black stone chips...

Twilight found him once again in the house of Dane, sitting over a bowl of boiled melde and nettle broth. The odor of the pungent greens rose in steam to his nostrils. By the flickering yellow light of a few tapers he once again observed the faces of the family. Their expressions

held now a certain weariness, but of the kind that seemed not burdening, but accepted. They seemed content with their labor, satisfied that in earning their daily bread…

His thoughts trailed off when he realized that Branwen was watching him. As he turned to her, she gave him a knowing smile that made him feel she could read his thoughts. It was somewhat upsetting to him, to have someone suddenly appear so close to the world he had been sure was his alone.

"Did you have a good day then?" Yetta was addressing him.

It took him a moment to collect himself. "Yes, a very good day."

Yetta nodded and smiled.

Dane looked up from his meal long enough to say, "We will wake you in the morning."

After that, no one spoke. The faintest whistling of wind could be heard through the cracks where the mud and dung daubing had failed away from the stick framework of the walls. The tapers flickered unevenly, as wooden spoons scraped softly on clay bowls.

Merlin, having taken his fill, drew his hands across the coarse raised grain of the table planks to the table's edge, and prepared to stand. He exchanged nods and glances with everyone, and then met Branwen's eyes. The light in her eyes made him smile. He rose, and walked across the room to the darkness of the stall. He wanted to turn and look once more at her, but was afraid she might be watching.

In the stall, moonlight glimmered on the hay. He gathered the straw into a pile and lay down on it. It was good to have a bed again, he thought. It was good to have that rest that each night seems to bring one on a different path to morning.

"Merlin. Wake up. We have much to do today."

Merlin turned his head and opened his eyes to see Branwen leaning over the half wall of the stall. Her face was in shadow, the only light in the room being the dim glow of the moon.

"What?"

"Come. The morning grows late."

"Late?" Merlin groaned.

But no response came forth; Branwen had already left. So be it, he thought. He threw the blanket from himself and stood, not yet awake. He blinked several times, as his eyes adjusted to waking sight. He shook his arms and legs, then picked up his cloak and draped it over his arm. Walking out to the main room, he found Branwen standing by the open hearth, stirring a cauldron of barley porridge. The low flames cast yellow and red tones over her face and arms. She smiled.

"Where is everyone?" Merlin asked.

"Come harvest, we have not the time to lie in bed sleeping until sunrise." She spoke with a mixture of insinuation and humor that surprised him. Had she guessed that he was high born? It was true: in his family it had not been common to wake before dawn, except for special rituals. Suddenly he felt out of place, but as she spoke more, the feeling quickly faded.

"I asked father if I might show you the village today."' She continued to stir the porridge, but smiled to herself.

"Oh? And what did he say?"

"Yes, for certain. We are usually wary of strangers, but Kendall has spoken well of you."

"Kendall? Is he one of the village elders?"

She looked into his eyes for a moment, and then gave a short laugh. "No, he is the young boy who sat with you by the bridge."

Merlin shook his head and laughed in return. "I did not know he would be your spokesman."

"One never knows," she offered.

They ate the barley from one bowl, standing close to the warmth of the fire. When they finished, Branwen carefully laid several stacks of small logs in rows upon the fire, then covered it all with large squares of turf.

"That should do until mother returns in the afternoon."

For a moment they stood close to one another, watching the fire and warming their hands on the flames, glancing up now and then to meet each other's eyes. Dawn broke. The first rays of yellow light poured through the eastern window and they walked out into the day.

The air was cool and misty, clear and sharp. Merlin drew a deep breath. The air nourished him, and the sunlight warmed his face. Now nothing concerned him but the moment's peace, as for the first time he felt the weight of his body pressing his feet to the ground. A few birds began to chirp loudly.

"This way," Branwen commanded, as she began to walk down the road.

He found it difficult to know when she spoke seriously, and when in jest. He followed her towards the low sun, towards the center of the village. He could see now the dark mounds of piled hay on their low platforms, dotting the outer pastures by the hundreds. A stray goat passed across their path.

They came now to the place of the firing. The round shallow pit had been dug and lined with dry straw. They watched as the dried pots were carefully laid in a mound in the center, and then covered with basketsful of dry wood and twigs. Larger and greener timbers were leaned against one another over the pit until the fire stood three feet high. Over all this fresh cut squares of turf were laid and the cracks between them filled with soil. A woman came with a flaming stick, and handed it to the fire builder.

"Merlin?" Branwen spoke his name as if to say, 'follow me.'

Merlin was momentarily startled, having been intently watching the fire making.

She brought him next to a line of large clay domes with small openings in the front. In one, a woman was feeding a fire of small charred sticks inside the dome. She went then to another, and raked out the hot embers. Merlin looked at Branwen questioningly.

"Watch," she said.

Five small loaves of bread were placed in the empty dome to bake. Merlin was embarrassed. Such things as bread had always been supplied to his house, and he had hardly ever gone into the village, preferring to be alone with his books and thoughts.

"With as much as you know, you could starve." Her words were true, and not unkind, but he withdrew from hearing them..

"But perhaps you will not," she added.

The morning had passed, quickly. Now as they walked on towards the outer fields, the sun had almost reached its highpoint in the sky. They passed close to the haystacks, covered with circular layers of thatched straw. They came to a huge rounded ledge of rock where the soil had washed away, leaving only a table of stone.

Several men were chipping away at the rock, standing in waist-deep holes as they worked to enlarge the outer walls of the holes; with mallets and chisels...

"These will be used to store the grains," Branwen explained.

Merlin looked at the men, their dark weather worn faces, their foreheads pouring: forth sweat. Thick muscles of arms, backs and shoulders rippled underneath brown skin as they worked.

He thought all of these tasks of great interest, but for certain this consuming labor could not be a way of

understanding. He looked over the near harvest fields where hundreds of workers stooped over the yellow grasses, or walked along swinging sickles. He saw in these people a living unto exhaustion; they held neither the inner reserve nor the capacity to undertake those more vital and longer journeys of life. They never ventured forth from the small worlds of their comings and goings, or the harsh necessities of earning their daily bread.

"Merlin, are you with me?" Branwen prodded him.

She led him to a shady place in the field, and they sat down. She looked at him in silence for a long time, and then spoke.

"You are different, Merlin, and you are the same. You may have vision to see from above, but you forget. The sea is still our common blood, and the soil the resting place for all our bones." She paused, and then continued, "Maybe you think they do not see, but they know in their own way. Their sweat is not the sweat of animals."

Merlin was astonished that someone could speak to his thoughts. Was she too alive as he so strived to be alive?

"And my work is unseen," he added.

He smiled at her, and took her hand in his. It was strangely tender for the hand of a laborer. The fingers were long and slender, and he let his fingers move over them. He looked into her eyes as though wanting to ask, who are you, where have you come from?'

She smiled back. "There are so few who would look into another's eyes, and say who and what they are."

Their eyes held one another's for a long moment, as the dry afternoon wind blew around them...

Through a worn spot in the thatched roof of the stall he could see the sky above him as he lay down. It was gray turning to black, with a few faint stars beginning to show.

What was it that stirred inside him? Perhaps the night would tell.

Sleep came over the village. Stars made their rounds in the night. It grew darker toward the midnight hour; at last the crescent moon began to rise. The night winds lingered soft and cool. The stars began to grow dim as the sky lost its blackness, washed out into gray.

On a distant hillside, a shadow swung a sickle, two cuts to every step. On the other slope, through the open windows of the houses, the lights of fires and candles appeared, one by one, as though brought by an invisible and swift-footed torchbearer, running down the trails, over the ridges, back and forth across the village, appearing on one side and then the other, without course, lighting houses in the village center, moving outward, moving in a great circle.. .

In Branwen's home, the family was gathering at the table. Dawn hung in the air around them, its warmth and light slowly filling the room. A pot of wheat and barley gruel cooked over the fire. Strips of leathery dried beef were piled on a wooden platter in the center of the table.

"Rudd, will you wake Merlin now?" Branwen asked, as she ladled the gruel into large bowls.

Rudd returned, surprised.

"He is not there," he said.

"What!?" Branwen exclaimed.

"He is gone," Rudd answered.

"Where?" She could not hide her anxiety. "Are his blankets still there?"

Rudd just shrugged his shoulders. Then he looked to his father, unsure of how to respond to Branwen's distress.

Dane gave him a reassuring smile.

Branwen laid down the bowls and rushed over to the stall. She let out a long breath. His blankets were there, one of them with a corner torn from it. She rushed back

through the front room, through the door into morning.

"Merlin?" She waited for a response.

"Merlin!" She called again.

A movement in the distance caught her eye, over on the harvest fields. Someone had already begun the day's labor, the hard pulling and swinging of the sickle, the making of sheaves. She looked closer. She recognized the unusual cloak, the long black hair waving over the shoulders.

She smiled a deep smile that was a soft joyous shout within her, and her eyes grew bright and full with her happiness. As she watched him she began to laugh, and could not stop.

When a few minutes later Ora came out to see what had become of her, she saw only two figures on the hillside, beginning a long and early day…

The silky threads of the sun in red emergence carried light down to the shoulders and backs of the long broken line of women in tattered shawls, and men in worn tunics. In peaceful march, the walkers came together as many small streams into a river, merging outside the village, moving slowly toward the hill where he and Branwen worked. They approached the outskirts of the field, and spread out once again over the hillside. Lowering their scythes and sickles from their shoulders, they each found the patch of waving yellow grass where work had ended for them the day before.

Those who came near, saw him, and nodded their heads approvingly amongst themselves. Soon all had found a place; they stood silently, facing the east. The red globe of the sun had now fully cleared the hilltops. Now in unison, a thousand pairs of arms were slowly lifted in salutation, with heads bowed toward the earth. The heads were lifted; a low wail began to resound in voices

all across the fields – *hih yiiiiiii-uh, hih yiiiiiii-uh*, then arms fell low with palms down – hi-yah!

The work began. The swinging of scythes and sickles moved to the rhythm of age old chants – *aydi aydi aydioh, a-ah-ahahhhdi, aydi aydi aydi-oh, a-ah-ahahhh-di*. Those pulling the long scythes cut wide swaths, moving slowly; those using the hand sickles made three or four cuts with every step. The children followed behind, skimming the cut grass off the top of the golden brown mat, and carrying it to carts when they had a full arm load.

Waves of wind undulated in the grass between the workers. The first hour passed, and thirst began to grow. One worker after another lifted an arm with open palm; to each a child came running with a gourd full of water dipped from the stream. Overhead, the sky lost its red, growing into a yellow amber. The sun climbed high into the sky with the pulse of human figures sweeping across the hillsides.

Soon hunger came; a small group broke off from the work to gather around the wicker baskets brought by the children. The eldest of the workers withdrew loaves of dark bread and large hunks of cheese from the baskets. Tearing the thick crusts of the loaves, he broke them into pieces, and passed them amongst the members of the group, who now sat around him in a circle. He did this also with the cheese.

When this group had finished, another group was brought the basket, so in any given area the rhythm of the work was not lost. It came Merlin's turn to eat. He did not join the group, but took only a gourd full of water from one of the children. Placing it up to his lips, he drank it slowly, letting it swish in his mouth, feeling its life in his throat. The rest he poured over his head; it ran dribbling over his face, bringing the salty taste of sweat to his lips. At this, the child who had given him

the gourd let out a big smile and giggled. Merlin smiled back. For a long time they stood smiling to each other, with the wind in their hair, and the sun on their faces, and there was nothing else. Merlin had no need to be Merlin, or the child, the child.

Merlin began to swing his scythe again; the child ran back to the stream with his empty gourd. All this time, Branwen was with him. Content to work beside him, she did not speak, but followed his strong and steady pace, yet wondering where he found his strength. The children ran around and around, their aprons over- flowing with grain, their arms filled with long grass.

Soon, hills of stalks and grain mounted by the dozen over the fields. The pace slowed, arms caressing the grain in a gentle stroking, but still steady, on and on. The sun had begun to fall; the long afternoon had begun. The workers shook sweat from the cloths they wore around their foreheads. They looked into the sun and prayed their work might carry through the day without slowing. They moved on, seemingly interweaving as they moved up hillsides, down into gullies, the fields growing low beneath their feet.

In the hottest part of the afternoon, a cool breeze began to blow. They thanked the creator's bounty, and were content, knowing they had his favor. Merlin was beginning to tire, but as he saw the sun dropping toward the horizon, and breathed in the cool wind, his strength was renewed. Once again he found the original pace of his work.

On and on through the afternoon the piles grew, the workers advancing, the sun falling low. The water brought by the children became food, became strength, and all that was needed. The day grew close to an end; their hearts were lightened, and songs began to fill the quietly stirring air.

The sun fell still lower, began to glow orange yellow,

then orange, then red. The work picked up, moving faster, dancing swifter and swifter, children running, the workers sweeping over the fields. The bottom edge of the deep red disc touched the distant hills to the west. The singing stopped, fell away into silence. Now standing, facing west, they listened and watched as the sun moved slowly below the hilltop. When the top edge disappeared, a great cry rose among them, filling the air, suddenly ending, leaving a few voices trailing into the twilight.

The sky soon turned gray; the flames of a hundred fires appeared in the cool darkening air over the hillsides, the burning of weeds and rotted straw. The streams of figures began to grow again, down the hillsides, into the valley. Clouds opened on the horizon to let a few golden rays pass across the gray sky; the air cooled. Now the fields were empty, except for the lone fire tenders.

But in the waving grass, the silhouette of two remained. They stood with their tools in their arms, facing each other. An invisible touch, a tender holding, passed between them. With that strength, their work began anew. They became shadows underneath the stars, glowing silhouettes beneath the rising moon.

The early hours of evening passed; at last the night called forth in its stillness to end their work. They turned to approach each other. Their eyes met; they stood motionless.

Branwen held her shoulders high and her arms crossed over her chest to hold herself warm from the now cold wind.

Merlin touched the top grains of the grass with his fingers, seeing her long hair trail outward into the wind, seeing her shining night blue eyes, and the gentlest smile on a weary flushed face of moonlight and shadow. Breathing hard and deeply, they held one another's seeing, held one another's bodies from afar, remembering, remembering precious life…

He watched as she poured one pot of steaming water after another from the fire into a wooden stave tub. In his exhaustion he could only sit and wait until the tub was filled. He threw his cloak onto the floor, and pulled the sweaty tunic off his body. He stepped into the hot soapy water scented with lavender flowers, feeling the heat up to his knees, with steam rising around him, his stiff muscles melting and unfolding into the hot liquidness. He lowered his body into a crouch, squatting on his heels, before finally lowering himself completely into the water. A slight stinging met his skin as he sat back, coming at last: to sit on the bottom of the tub.

He leaned back with his knees up. The water's gift of heat drew the stiffness from his muscles; he let them fall into their own softness, and breathed deeply as he exhaled a long relaxing moan. The soap and lavender cleansed the sweat from his pores, soothing his skin.

She had filled the tub by the light of a torch, and then had left with it. Now it seemed a soft ethereal light was growing in the room.

He rested his head on his shoulder, and closed his eyes, too weary to think, too awake to dream. The warmth surrounded his body, and his breath nourished him, carrying life throughout his body. He rubbed his skin once over with a coarse cloth, then fell motionless again, not stirring for a long time.

When he felt he had fully received the water's healing, he stood slowly up in the tub. The cool air touched his skin: He bent down to pick up a bucket of cold water, and then splashed it over himself with his hand, as he shook and let out a soft shout. The sharp chill ran over his chest and back; he rubbed himself with both hands.

He stepped out, reaching for a large wiping cloth, then sat on a wooden bench. The wood was smooth on his thighs, its surface worn through the years. And as he sat watching the steam rise off his body, he could feel on the

soles of his feet the flat stones that had been pressed into the earth to make a floor. His eyes traced their crooked pattern over to the corner where his cloak and leather sandals lay strewn, like crumpled shadows of his journey.

The room was now aglow; he saw for the first time the candle that burned behind the tub. In the fading moonlight and deeper darkness of early morning, it seemed to glow more brightly. He took it in his hand and went to Branwen. Its flame cast a copper light on her long slender white form and sleek legs, moving over the bed naked to slip, like a cat, under the blankets.

He put the candle beside the bed, and kneeled over her, placing his knees and face against hers. He listened to her, and to his own life, trying in a moment to touch that place of deepest silence within himself. He sat back on his heels, as with outstretched arm she lifted the covers for him so that he could crawl in to lie beside her. He caught a glimpse of her small smooth rounded breasts, and the dark triangle between her thighs. He lay down, curling up to her, and she to him.

Between their eyes, a silent word passed, like a wind that swept from their day, from themselves as they lay, to their own infancy, and back to the child that now lay unborn between their bodies. Merlin turned over to blow out the light of the candle. The night sky returned to the room through the small window.

He could see now the outlines of her face, the fine lips and small chiseled nose, the darkness of her large eyes. He moved his hand so their hands were palm to palm; he ran one finger over her palm. He pushed her fingers with his, feeling their motion, and the slight resistance of their muscles. He held a loosely cupped hand over the tops of her fingers, and then lowered his hand to press the soft fleshy pads of his fingertips against hers, and caress their smoothness.

He moved a knee against her knee, and gently kissed the center of her palm. She smiled, and moaned softly.

"I am so tired," she said. ""Is it all alright?

"Yes," he smiled softly, "It's alright."

Where now was the rage in his bones and blood? He listened; he could still make out its pulse. But mostly there was a warmth in his chest, and a lightness in his eyes and head, a momentary peace to be near her.

She was drifting into sleep now, leaving him alone with the stars, the few that he could see glimmering through the narrow window.

Merlin woke up, opening his eyes to look over her shoulder at her still closed eyes. She stirred, as though feeling his gaze. She opened her eyes, turned and looked into his.

They shared a soft silent smile. She turned over onto her back.

After a moment she asked, "Do you hear the rain, Merlin?"

"Yes?"

"Do you hear the raindrops?" she asked.

He nodded.

"Can you hear three different kinds of raindrops? Listen. Some hit the window ledge, some splatter on the wet leaves, and some splash in the puddles."

Merlin propped himself up on an elbow, turning an ear toward the window.

"No, no," Branwen said, pulling his arm gently out from underneath him. "Just be calm, and let the listening come. Then you will hear them."

He listened for a moment, but could not tell whether he was hearing them or not.

"Oh, do not mind," she whispered as she kissed his forehead and left the bed, "we have another full day before us."

They dressed and walked out to the hearth. The sun had been up for several hours; everyone had left long ago. They took porridge from the pot over the fire. Merlin took his bowl to a corner of the room and sat down, as some thoughts of his previous days returned to him. He was readying himself to sink into a morning of peaceful contemplation when Branwen called.

"Merlin, come here."

"What is it, Branwen?" he asked.

"Come help me with the bread."

He walked over to the table where she stood. She took a large slab of dough from her bowl, tore it in half, and slapped it down on the table in front of him. She looked him in the eye, and pointed with a doughy finger to the bread dough.

"Knead it!" she commanded.

"But I have never done it before," he protested.

Branwen pointed again, jabbing her finger in the air. "Knead it!"

Merlin shrugged his shoulders and smiled sheepishly. He cautiously moved his hands toward the sticky mass, pushing at it with his fingertips. Branwen laughed. His hands jumped back. She laughed again, delighted.

"Here, I will show you." She picked up her pile of dough, and with a dramatic flourish, threw it high into the air. It sailed between the wooden rafters and fell back down onto the table. She looked out of the corner of her eye to see if she had made the intended impression on him. She could see that it had.

She placed the heels of her hands together on the dough, and pushing it forward with all her weight, flattened it out. She turned a third of it back upon itself, pushing again, and again, developing a strong and steady rhythm.

Suddenly she stopped and looked over to him. He opened his eyes wider, questioning.

"Now you do it," Branwen said.

He nodded his head and smiled.

Taking his dough between his hands, he heaved it upward. It bounced off a low part of the roof, and landed momentarily on the crossbeam.

He watched in dismay as it began to sag and stretch into two pieces, until its weight pulled it free of the beam. He lunged to one side to catch the first piece between his arms and stomach, while the other piece landed with a thud on the wooden floor.

Branwen was laughing uncontrollably.

He looked at her, wondering if she was making jest of him, but then realized it did not matter.

He began to laugh, and they both laughed, laughing more and more deeply.

Sunlight poured through the eastern window, warming them.

Branwen took his hands in hers, and pushed them into the dough. She stood behind him, leaning with him as he moved, showing him how to use his body weight to make a circular rhythm with his hands.

She returned to her place, and they kneaded side by side. It seemed to him one of the happiest moments of his life, and tears came to his eyes from a joy he knew could not last…

He spent the remainder of the morning speaking with the village people. When afternoon came, he wandered toward the outer pastures. He found a quiet shaded place, and lay down in the tall grass.

He felt everything to be moving swiftly around him; something was happening not of his own choosing. He could no longer hold to his path of learning.

He wanted to struggle, to find some way to return, but the sun was too clear, and the wind too gentle, and the earth too strong.

The few clouds above him stirred in the high winds, and painted changing forms in strokes of white and gray on the blue sky. He watched the sun falling slowly toward the horizon, and listened to the wind in the grass, and the calling of skylarks overhead. He felt on his arms the dampness of the soil, and smelled the now rotting leaves that had fallen from the tree above him. His thoughts blew over and around him, but none could take root; none could find him.

The afternoon grew late. He sat up to see the low sun coloring the lake water gold. He wanted to be closer. He walked back down the trail of bent grass he had made, until he came near to the water.

He stepped in small steps closer to the lakeshore, where the water became an ever more transparent covering until finally drawing its fine curving line on the small stones, and wetting others with the slightest of rippling, only enough to make them shine in the sunlight. Overhead, the pale blue sky was daubed in light gray, and brushed in white with the lightest of strokes. The sun like a great thirty-armed star was dropping low in the late afternoon sky.

He squatted on his heels, looking out over the water. From the distant shore he could hear the sound of children playing, carrying across the water. Where now was his search? At times it seemed of no consequence, and he needed only to join the peace he could feel around him.

The first winds of evening picked up, blowing the water to pulse gently on the shore. He watched a large flat rock that protruded above the water, as it seemed to grow and diminish with the water's movement, alive, breathing. His hands hung loose on his knees, and he looked at his face in the lake's reflection.

Another face appeared over his; Branwen kneeled down silently beside him. He saw her high cheekbones

and arched brows in the water; between the ripples he looked again at her tender lips. He turned toward her to see her long golden white hair lifted by the wind into a wave blowing away from her slender neck, but still touching her shoulders. For a moment he looked into her eyes, hoping to see in them the least glimmer of changing light that would tell him she understood. He watched for the slightest trembling of her lips that would tell him she knew his love.

He looked back across the water. Two ducks lifted themselves from the lake, flapping their wings inches above the water in a long gliding trail, calling *whee-oo whee-oo.* The sun was dim now, just above the treetops.

...that year the wheat harvest came late. Each morning the elder came to the field, just after the dew had dried. He picked a few grains from the grass, then bit through them carefully and slowly. But each day he would shake his head, and the anxious workers would return to their other labors. The grains were still too soft and would not grind well into flour. When they were ready they would become hard all the way through. Then not an hour could be wasted, because when the grains had so matured, they might fall from the ears and be lost in the first strong gusting of wind.

At last the day came; the work began, the entire population of the village laboring together. The grain was harvested and placed in the storage pits. The straw was cut later and bundled into sheaves tied with twisted straw ropes, to be used for thatching, bedding and animal feed. The land was plowed with oxen teams to prepare for the coming spring; many hours were spent raking manure from carts and sledges onto the freshly turned soil. The last of the vetch and melde crops were brought into the enormous sheds; now little work remained in the fields.

They began to prepare for the cold rains of winter. The wool was spun into yarn, and woven into warm clothes. New thatching was laid on the roofs, and the buildings secured against the elements. Oak, ash and elm trees were cut a stockpiled to provide heat for the cold days ahead.

Winter came, and the woodlands had need of tending. The hazel trees were cut every year to ensure a supply of rods to be made into baskets, fences, and thatching spars. Amongst the hardwoods, special natural shapes were sought out to make the strongest tools, a forked branch for a pitchfork, a curving bough for a plow beam, with the grain running with the contour of the tool. The year's supply of implements was carefully seasoned over the long burning winter hearths.

During these months, Merlin shared in the work, and was well accepted by all. He remained sleeping in the stall; he had helped to give it new thatching, thicken the walls, and build a wooden platform for his bed. During the day he was usually out in the woodlands helping to gather fuel. At night the family ate together, and then gathered around the hearth to share skills, crafts and stories.

It was during these times that Merlin learned of the good hearts of these people, and of the village elders, and of their ancestors before them, who had settled the village six generations ago. He learned of the battles that had been fought against the raiders from the eastern sea. This was a peaceful time now; some seventeen years had passed since those unfriendly tribes had found the river passage that led up into this remote valley.

The months passed from the deep of winter, the skies grew brighter, the days longer. Branwen and Merlin, who had now shared many warm evenings together at home in the company of all the family, were once again

able to find some time to be alone together in the fields. Their friendship had deepened, and they were able to share those things closest to their hearts as they roamed over the hillsides. It was in the early part of May, during one of these walks that Branwen spoke to Merlin about the journey he was on.

"Merlin?"

"Yes?"

"Do you want a home?" she asked.

"I am afraid I do not know what that is...is it a place? Is it love? Is it a woman, or maybe, a way of peacefully moving through the seasons?"

"It is all of these," she answered.

"Perhaps, but not for me. I feel I have only one home – it is that strength and courage that surrounds me when I know I am doing what I have been given to do."

"Then have faith and your home is well secured." She seemed not happy with his answer, adding "I see that it is not for me to give you that which other men seek."

"Somewhere within me I, too, seek those same things, and yet I know I can not hope for them."

Branwen stopped walking, and looked into his eyes. She laid her hand on the side of his cheek. "You will be alone, Merlin, alone beyond all imagining.'

He stopped, "Yes, and that too will be my power."

The wind was blowing gently now. High above a hawk beat the air in long strokes, and soon passed into the blue deepness of the sky.

"You are going to leave, Merlin?"

"I am sorry, Branwen."

"I will go with you," she stated.

"You know it can not be. Your place is with your family," he said, wanting it to be true.

"My place is with the family I choose," she answered.

"If only...no, Branwen…" he stopped himself from saying more, or hoping more…

She began to weep, letting her hand fall from his face, and spoke in broken breaths. "Merlin, there is a place, so fine and tender a place, that comes to us so rarely, in which we know each other, and touch and feel our aliveness, that when we return from it, we can not remember, we can not even imagine it to be there, but yet we think it is still ours to possess, even as it grows ever more distant from us. And we can say, yes, we remember, and yes, yes, to those who try to tell us of this place, but in truth we are so far from it that it does not move us in the least to speak of it, to say yes, I know what it is you speak of, or yes, your words are true, but really we do not remember, and we are left alone with only our words." She turned and ran weeping down the hillside, toward thc village.

"Branwen!'" He called after, not knowing what to say or do. He watched her disappear, and then sat down to wait for the sunset. When after a time, he finally began to walk down the hillside, the trails were deserted.

This was the night of the spring festival. He joined the people gathered in the village center. At last the procession came, a hundred torches carried around and around, and up and down, appearing as great interwoven wreathes of light in the dark evening air. Walking in a large circle, they moved slowly at first, accompanied by a rhythmic chant, and the hitting of hollow logs on stones.

A wail began, a long low wail, increasing in loudness. The witch of winter came forth, a stuffed figure with a bizarre painted face, draped in black clothes and held on the end of a long pole. In and out she ran, through the crowd, through the circle, faster and faster, the wail growing ever louder. As she ran past Merlin, her eye seemed to glare in the firelight, coming alive, meeting his gaze. She climbed the great bonfire. Two men and two women rushed forth from the directions of the four winds to light the fire. The flames grew around her; the

wail became almost a scream; the fire caught her clothes, began to consume her. As she crumpled into the flames, the crowd gave a loud shout of joy and raised up their arms. Each man chose a woman to dance; they swirled round and round, lifting their feet, kicking them over the ground with a swing of a knee. The smell of burning hay filled the air.

A young woman suddenly grabbed Merlin, swinging him around and around. The entire scene became a circling blur of color, until neither of them could stand without holding on to each other. The world began slowing to a stop in a tilted swirling, and she disappeared again into the crowd.

Two huge staved barrels of beer arrived on the back of pony drawn carts. Soon everyone danced with a full mug in their hand as they returned again and again to the barrels for more. The flames flickered on their already red faces laughing and shouting and huffing for breath. The dancing would go on until dawn.

He returned at midnight to find her sitting before the hearth. He sat down beside her and opened his palms to the heat of the flames. The red embers crackled and the wood smelled of cherry. After a time he began to speak to her, and to the fire.

"I must go; there is something ahead of me, something that calls to me. I don't know. Darkness is there too. But I know if I go – when I go – I must go with no thought of returning, of ever coming back to the life I know, or to those who know me, because I do not know who it is that will be returning." He stopped for a moment, gathering his thoughts, letting the fire speak… "To truly set out, there must be no ties to the past, no tether that marks a boundary of my wandering, even though the chain be golden and fine as gossamer. It will be another that returns as me. I can make no promises; this is best."

Branwen was weeping softly now, but he continued.

"You see, another doorway has come to me. These doorways come in many ways, appearing only when one is worthy; I live my life for that worthiness. For others perhaps, they are sometimes seen, sometimes not, sometimes approached, sometimes fled. They are the sum total of life's offerings, its very blood." Branwen listened, silently now. "I have never turned from a doorway. I have always watched them, opened them, entered. But now I am hesitating; there is something different this time. The door before me opens not only into an unknown room, but to a room not of my house. I can not even imagine what could lie behind it. I am not frightened, but I am unsure." She moved closer to him, laying his head against her breast. "

"It seems that once before I gave my life to pass through, and awakened to find a new life waiting. But now this life I must leave is longer and fuller yet. All those I deeply love have come to me in this time. It has been many years. Now again, I leave. If I hesitate, it is because there is so much more here to leave behind. But I will go through. I will go through. It is my only way of living, as it seems there is no end to dying."

Neither of them spoke for a long time; they listened to the sound of their own breathing, and to the whispering of the embers. Branwen searched within herself to find something to say. Words came, in a clear and soft tone, from an unknown place.

"It is the miracle of love that in giving our lives to our loved ones, we give to our loved ones, their own lives as well." Branwen left him by the fire, and went into her-room. After a few moments, she called to him.

He pushed open the heavy door into her room. On a pile of furs, against the orange glow of a well-bedded fire she lay outstretched on her back, one foot upon her knee, and her hands by her sides. Her skin made a pastel

mirror for the flickering fire colors. Her breasts were full and upraised, with dark centers. He sat down beside her, sharing a soft smile, watching the play of light in her eyes.

She slipped her hand under his, palm to palm. She turned his other hand over and held on to the fingers; she traced the lines in his palm with her fingertip. She turned the other hand up, examining both of them closely. Suddenly, as he watched her, her eyes became his, and for the first time in his life he saw his own hands; they were gentle hands, with long fingers.

He touched her eyelids with his fingertips, moved down her cheeks to gently part her lips, down her throat, palm curving over on breast, over the smooth soft belly, into her thighs, resting, covering fully with his hand the soft furrow. Then he drew back.

What was holding him back? "No, I cannot," he whispered, "forgive me the desire in my touch, but your love is not an easy thing in my solitude. Something in me cries out for you, but I know this will bring me no closer to what I seek. At most it could only be a momentary peace in my flight to what lies ahead. It is not that I – do not weep, Branwen…"

"Where are you, Merlin?"

"I do not know, Branwen. I do not know."

She nodded, accepting.

He lay back on the furs with her, and they held each other. He moved his head back to see her face.

Her tears were running down in the hollows under her eyes, across her cheeks. They formed tiny droplets on her eyelashes that shone like crystals in the flame light.

He ran his fingers across the tips of her eyelashes, making the droplets sparkle in the slightest of movements.

"Rest, Merlin, you will need your rest," she said kindly, before falling asleep in his arms.

He looked over her naked form into the darkness, trying to see something he knew was there, had to be there.

...as he traced his finger along the downward curve of her hip, her flesh seemed to dissolve before his eyes, and in the darkness he could see only a skeleton beside him, with the web of a spider growing over the ribcage -- his body jerked and he gasped. He felt the warmth of her body and heard her breathing.

There was still weariness in him when his eyes opened to a room slowly giving its darkness to morning gray to muted yellow, but there was hope, too. And as he watched the first streams of dawn light entering through the narrow window, in rays made solid by the dusty air, he knew there was a greater life waiting.

Now, as the colors of the cloth on Branwen's loom grew bright in the morning light, he could see that it was the sun that lent its beauty to her weaving. This one would be an earthen blanket, in subtle tones of red and brown and yellow. The blanket covering them was of the warmest red; the looping of yarn over the beams shone in many shades of green.

The morning grew still brighter; the day would be clear.

He turned on his side, propping himself up on an elbow. Beside him, Branwen was still curled on her side, her cheek resting on a pillow of one hand palm downward on the other. She was breathing softly through slightly pursed lips. Looking at her long eyelashes and delicate nose, and the near translucent skin pulled over high cheekbones, he thought how much she seemed like a child, and yet was more a woman to him than any other he had ever known. He wondered if another man would ever touch her so deeply, or if she might come to know herself as deeply as he had known her.

He began to dress and gather his bags. When he was ready to leave, he approached her again, stooping down to kiss her white forehead. She stirred, but did not awaken. He though it best to not disturb her peace, so he closed his eyes to speak silently to her.

"Branwen, I am leaving you, wishing I could have given you so much more, but knowing I will hold you again one day."

He went out into the morning. The sun was lifting itself from a bed of red and gold wispy clouds on the eastern hills. The wind swirled, cool enough to refresh, warm enough to embrace. Small raindrops were falling yards apart from a clear blue sky that held but a few white clouds overhead. A silhouette of long curving wings swooped before him. A bird called, *ke-wick, kewick, ke-wick.*

The Mountain
and
The Chapel

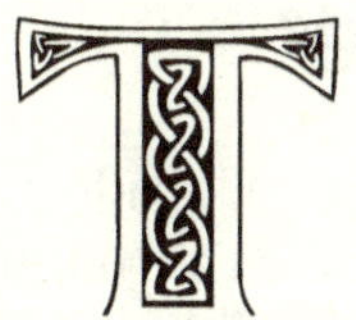

he amber seeds are trembling, trembling on fine branches atop golden stalks of field grass, trembling stalk to stalk in the in the hidden wanderings of the still air. Each stirring of wind marks like a breath their life's passage, recording the minutes as hours. In the great arc of the sun across the afternoon sky, another year completes itself. In four seasons a generation passes. One decade marks the term of history, beyond which lie the unknown millennia.

The amber seeds are trembling, and none have heard the tale of Macsen Wledig. Their distant ancestors would have told them how one man rose in the later times of the Roman occupation to be declared emperor by the combined legionnaires and tribes of the British island. He fought his way to Rome under the banner of the Red Dragon, and ruled the imperial city for five years, before falling in battle.

And those ancestors were still decades from seed when the Romans established here two great fortresses, Isca to the south, and Dera to the north. Each held six thousand men of the shortsword.

The amber seeds are trembling, and perhaps can still feel across the countless terms of history, the fearsome rumblings of the earth beneath them. Some four centuries ago, their most ancient ancestors were trodden underfoot by the great army of the eastern continent. The Romans assembled the most awesome military power ever known. With its superbly trained and disciplined ranks it laid claim to all of the known world. The Romans came to Britain and conquered the tribes of the east, then gathered at the foot of the mountains that led into the western regions. On the other side, the tribes of the Silurians and Ordovicans assembled, along with all those who considered peace with Rome another name for servitude. The tribesmen were fearless, led by the Brythonic warrior prince Caradog. But the military wealth and training of the Roman army was without equal, and the tribes were at last beaten. Caradog was taken prisoner with many others, then paraded through the streets of Rome, and led before the emperor.

Caradog alone was greater than misfortune; he walked with neither fear nor sorrow, nor condescension; he behaved with dignity amidst ruin.

He spoke to the emperor in this manner: 'Ambitious Rome aspires to universal dominion. Must all mankind, therefore, bend their necks to the yoke? I stood at bay for years – had I acted otherwise where would have been your glory of conquest? Where would have been my honor of brave resistance?'

And the amber seeds still hold an ancient memory, for no life can ever forget a bath of innocent blood, and the rain cannot wash it from the soil. Two decades later the resistance was broken.

The Romans went to Anglesey, where the good Druids lived and worked, kind and gentle men, teachers, priests, seers, courageous and wise men they were. They were the voice and vision of the tribes, of the unborn nation. The Romans went to Anglesey and cut their throats. They burned the sacred groves of oaks, so that darkness descended on the people of the tribes, and their hearts were made weak.

A few of the Druids escaped, by the grace or perhaps the penance of God. They had been tending the sacred books and treasures in a remote part of the valley. They alone survived the massacre, and were its witnesses, fated to live on with its memory.

When they saw what had befallen their beloved companions, they gathered up the treasures, and carrying them in wicker baskets strapped to their backs, ran deep into the hills. In the region of Llwyn Cerrig Bach, they themselves dispersed, never to see one another again…

This last night, the wind had wrapped him in its subtle fury, and now this morning, a light fog hovered between the hills. The drizzle had thoroughly wet his blankets. The chill and dampness was on his body, and the ground beneath him had suddenly grown cold and inhospitable. He stood up, not yet awake, or fully rested.

For many hours he climbed the trail upward. When he reached the first ridge, he looked far across the land. A few jagged peaks rose high above the mists, behind the lower horizon of forested hills. Above their green tops black rock and fields of white silver snow lay on the highest slopes. In the sky, the clouds made one great waving sheet of white and gray flame moving upward, with thin streams of blue barely visible.

The trail led him by a mountain lake. He stopped to drink. The wind rose up, blowing fiercely, and the clouds darkened overhead. In another moment, the air became still. Snowflakes fell, their perfect crystals reflected in a cerulean blue mirror. Touching the water, the icy whiteness of their forms glowed, and then vanished. He remained still on his side, leaning over the water's edge.

He saw reflected in the water the rock outcropping of an eastern ridge, its massive gray blocks laid one upon the other. The stone climbed back into the hills several thousand feet, disappearing into the earth's depths near the crest of the ridge. Perhaps there he might find a suitable ledge on which he could build a fire to warm himself and dry his clothes. He climbed several hundred feet up the hillside. Only a little farther up, he spotted a cave, pieces of charred log at its entrance.

"Hail!" He called into the cave, listening for a response. Nothing stirred. The fog had closed in around him; now the ledges would be too dangerous to descend. He entered. As he stepped through the opening, the ground suddenly dropped down a foot, and he stumbled forward

with the momentum of the unexpected step. His foot caught on a spur of rock, and he fell headlong into a globular cavern. As he pushed himself back up onto his knees, he noticed the room was barely lit. He looked around until he saw a wick glowing in a bowl dug into the rock wall, as his sight grew clearer in the darkness. Now we could see the almost imperceptible flickering of the flame's glow on the cavern floor.

He stood up and walked over to the flame. The wick was set in a brownish liquid that collected in the bottom of the bowl after dribbling down the rock. He dipped a finger into it. It was slippery between his fingers.

There was a small ring of stones in the center of the floor, and more pieces of charred log. Cupping his hand, he threw some of the liquid on the pieces. Then he ripped a scrap of coarse cloth from his carrying bag, and carried a flame to the log. As the flames spread he piled the pieces to build a growing fire. He sat down cross-legged, feeling the soft heat on his knees and outstretched palms.

He closed his eyes, thinking of Branwen, traveling back to her side – the sound of stirring rock came from the cave entrance. He opened his eyes, and was blinded. The air was lit with an intense brilliance that caused him to squint in pain. He opened his eyes again, slowly. Color exploded from every surface of the cave, gold, red, silver, blue and green, filling his mind with its flickering. The flames grew low again; the colors dimmed.

In the entrance of the cave, he saw the silhouette of a man, with his feet planted apart, and his arms hanging down at his sides. He stood motionless in the light of the now dim sun. And then he was gone from sight.

"So you have come, Merlin." The voice from the back of the cave startled Merlin. He turned around to see an old man stepping from the shadows. His long white hair hung down over his shoulders, but on top was wispy and

thin so the hair on the sides seemed to grow from a ring around the crown of his head. He stepped closer.

Their eyes met. His eyes were dark, but lighted from within, reflecting, but of great depth. They spoke of time, of journeys. Merlin lost himself, unable to speak.

"Did you come with any food?" the old man asked.

"What?" was the only thing Merlin could say, jolted from his reverie.

"Not so hard a question! Let us have it then," the old man insisted, looking to Merlin's bag.

Merlin dug in his bag for a small pouch of mixed grains, and then handed it cautiously to the old man. The old man took it in his hand with a smile and walked to the entrance of the cave. He made a chattering noise with his teeth and tongue, and called, "Kenedyr." A large red squirrel scampered over the ground to him. He emptied a small pile of the grains onto the ground. The squirrel ate happily, and allowed the man to stroke his fur.

"An old friend indeed," he mumbled, "but I have not had anything to give him for such a long time now."

He looked up to Merlin, who had followed him outside.

"I am called Ioin."

"And I am Merlin, as you seem to know – but how?"

Ioin chuckled to himself. "You look tired and should rest. You can unroll your blankets near the fire."

Somehow, Merlin already trusted him, and so did as he was told. At first he was too excited to sleep, but his exhaustion soon overcame him.

When he awoke, it was twilight, and he went outside. It was then that he first heard it. In the total silence of the fog-laden air, a bell sounded, carrying its note clear and far, and faded slowly. It rang again; it filled the valley with its voice. It came from above.

Ioin appeared beside him, and listened too. "What is it?" Merlin asked.

Ioin grew somber. "It is the bell of Llwyn Cerrig Bach. It is heard sometimes on nights when an unknown danger is approaching. No one has ever seen it, though many have spent years searching." He turned to face Merlin. "You have a warrior's eyes, but your heart is pure, and not lacking courage."

"I do not want to be a warrior," Merlin said.

"And yet you have been chosen, though it is not what you imagine. A true warrior is not a violent man. When others are killed, he weeps over them in sorrow. When he is victorious in war, he observes the rites of mourning. He knows the realm of death as well as that of life, and so cannot be destroyed. He chooses to fight always on the One Side, so life does not desert him."

"But why join arms at all?" Merlin asked.

It is not a joining, but a giving that overcomes. There was a time when so many of us sought the way of peace that we furthered the goals of violent men. The empire cannot be so defended; the way of peace cannot be left so naked. The One Will must appear everywhere, even if it is in the shining of a newly forged sword – come with me."

Ioin scurried down the hill into the forest surrounding the lake. Merlin found him collecting yellow flowers. "Chamomile, Merlin. We will sleep well tonight." When they returned to the cave, Ioin brewed the flowers into an aromatic tea. They drank it slowly.

"Do you collect many other herbs?" Merlin asked.

"Oh yes, all kinds. Tomorrow we will forage."

Merlin nodded, uncertain of Ioin's purpose.

Finishing their tea, they watched the low flames of the fire grow into red embers. Then they retired.

They spent the next day in the fields and in the forest. He taught Merlin where to look for dozens of different kinds of plants, how to identify them, and how to prepare the different parts, leaves, roots, seeds and flowers. Some were to be used as medicines, some as food, some as poisons, and even some for braiding into rope.

Merlin was most excited about the medicines, but Ioin warned him against depending solely on these remedies. "Remember it is the spirit that heals in all ways; it alone is the guide. The herbs I teach you are only gifts to bring you closer to the inner strength. For even one breath of air fully drawn can heal all affliction, and one draught of running water reverently taken can soothe any suffering. The trees themselves would give you their life and wisdom could you only humble yourself before them."

As the days grew into weeks, Merlin's knowledge increased but he understood Ioin less and less. One day Merlin was sitting on the rocky ledge of the lake shore, when Ioin appeared, and stood behind his shoulder. He did not say anything or look at him. The reflections of both their faces shined in the still water. Ioin smiled; Merlin saw it on the water and smiled back. Ioin smiled bigger; he smiled bigger. Ioin lifted his eyebrows. Merlin questioned back with his, becoming very amused. There came a gentle but forceful push against his back, and he fell head first into the picture. A shock passed through his body as the cold water surrounded him, and a moment of darkness as he tried to find the surface. He broke through into the air and gasped.

Ioin stood above him in utmost seriousness. "There is no reflection, in mind, in dream, in feeling or thought that is apart from what seems to be real. All these bring the world to be, and are equally real wherever they appear. Only you can choose those you will live within, and those you will discard."

Merlin had nothing to say. It was his own fault to have placed himself in such a vulnerable position on that

ledge. Ioin offered him a hand, pulling him out of the water. Then he winked at Merlin, who twisted his mouth into a reluctant smile.

Near the end of the month, they started a garden in the lower valley. It was a fair distance, and they could tend it only every other day. It was while returning alone from the garden one day that Merlin heard the bell again. The wind was strong, blowing in from the south; the bell's ringing floated in steps down the valley.

When he returned to the cave, he again asked Ioin about it. Ioin looked at him intently. "What do you hear now?"

Merlin listened but could hear nothing. "Nothing, nothing at all."

"This is why you do not understand. Do you think silence is simply silence?" He did not wait for an answer. "There is silence that holds danger to be smelled, wisdom to be heard, silence that paints visions to be seen, that carries air to be touched... there is silence of thunder, of grass in the wind, silence of stones, silence that is story, that is song, silence in the cry of a bird, silence that embraces, that casts away, that loves, that hates, silence too great to be heard."

The wind ruffled Ioin's hair. Merlin listened. A sound came, a sound within him. It grew ever more present until it filled his mind and body. A light stirred in his eyes and his fingertips tingled. His own strength became one with the strength of the wind.

The gusting wind grew calm again. And Merlin knew now something had come to him in this moment, but he did not know yet what it was.

And there was much more to occupy his mind. Ioin called him one evening into the back of the cave; he slid away a large standing slab of rock, revealing a

small passageway. Taking a torch down from the wall, he entered into the rock, motioning for Merlin to follow him. They crawled through the tunnel to a small chamber.

In the middle of it was a small chest, which Ioin opened. Inside there were about thirty large leather-bound manuscripts. He began to take them out, and then stopped, looking to Merlin. "I will tell you," he said, blowing the dust off a cover, "I have not opened any of these in a long time, but I think you might find them of interest...one thought however: my own teacher Marcas never held much faith in books. He asked me one day, 'Ioin, if the wise are called the wise, who calls them so?' Of course he answered it himself. 'It is the unwise, fashioning wisdom according to their own judgments. Among some the man knowledgeable in horse trading is called wise; among others the man who knows how to waylay a traveler. This is no different with the men of books. They all have their own needs, recognized or not, and call wisdom what suits them best.' So I give this warning to you, Merlin. If you would truly learn the power of the way, you must by your own will let life remake you to its own design. And let no man perceive you on the way, lest he fill your mind with doubt, and cast the Sea of Mind upon you, even as you are trying to climb away from its shores."

Merlin listened, but remained anxious to discover what sacred knowledge was kept in these ancient parchments. Ioin looked at him with understanding, remembering his own thirst for knowledge.

"Well here, open them," said Ioin, handing him a pile of books."

Merlin opened them one after another. The first described the science of the stars and heavens. The next outlined military campaigns and strategy, another a treatise on edible plants and medicinal herbs. Still

another explained how to forecast weather changes And languages, ancient languages.

Much excited by this storehouse of knowledge, Merlin spent his summer months studying under Ioin's guidance. His mind filled with new ideas. He read twelve and fourteen hours a day, as though driven by some inner force.

And still he had to find time to keep up with his labors. It was while working at one of these tasks, in the month of September, that his training took another unexpected turn.

He was out in the fields. He had filled a natural basin of rock with barley grains, and with another round stone was working hard at grinding them into flour. He sat cross-legged, his head bent over the stone.

Ioin came quietly up the trail, and sat down unnoticed about thirty feet behind him. He poured a small pool of water into the dirt from a vase he carried, and then scraped in some loose dirt to form a thick mud. He smiled as he looked at the back of Merlin's head, and began shaping the mud into clumps. When he had about twelve of them he put six in his left hand, and one in his right. Then he stood. Taking aim several inches to the side of Merlin's ear, he shouted, "Merlin!"

Merlin turned to see a clump of mud sailing in front of his face. He jerked his head back and gasped.

"Defend yourself," Ioin yelled, hurling the mud clumps in quick succession at his head, feet, chest, arms and legs. But each time he gave Merlin barely time to crouch, jump, or turn out of the way. Ioin was having great fun, laughing at Merlin's distress. Merlin turned his back to run to the shelter of some boulders, but now Ioin unleashed his remaining clumps in all his power and accuracy.

He felt the wet stinging on his head, and the back of his legs. "To run from battle in haste strengthens your

enemy and weakens yourself!" Ioin intoned.

Enough of this foolish preaching, old man. Merlin bent over to pick up some clods of dirt. But suddenly in a few strides Ioin covered the distance between them, and Merlin realized an instant too late that he had turned his side to the enemy. Ioin ran into him at full speed, butting Merlin's bottom with his shoulder, and sent him sprawling across the dirt.

"If your offense has not been prepared, you must weaken your enemy by defense alone!"

Cursed old man, Merlin thought, always right, as he picked himself up from the ground.

From then on it was war, and Merlin always found himself on the defensive. Wherever he was Ioin would find him. Whenever he tried to find some quiet place for himself, Ioin would appear. When Merlin grew confident in his ability to evade the slings of mud that constantly whipped by him, Ioin began to use small stones. These were much harder to see, and Merlin had to concentrate to see one coming, while at the same time not focusing his vision so narrow that he would miss the next one that would surely follow. It became a dangerous dance of jumping, crouching, swirling and turning, shifting to one side and then the next, his balance never stationary, ever ready to move, and yet superbly poised. His eyes and ears grew instantly responsive, until his movement became instinct. Whether sitting, lying or walking he maintained his awareness, lest Ioin should suddenly appear from behind a rock or bush to let loose a shower of missiles against him.

Often at the end of his days, he found himself counting his bruises. He never rested or stopped anywhere without considering his defense in the surroundings. But he grew too confident.

One day he carefully disappeared from Ioin, making sure he was not followed. He climbed to the edge of a deep ravine, and then slid down into it. At last, he thought, I can have a few hours of peace.

Moments later Ioin appeared, a shadow on the ridge above him. The sun glared behind him. Merlin realized the stones would be invisible against the sunlight. He quickly made the visual scan of the territory he should have made when he first came.

"Shall I spare your life, young fool?" Ioin called down.

He needed more time. He stalled. "How have I wronged you, oh mighty one?" Every way of escape brought him closer to Ioin's threat, except one. A short way down, the ravine fell a sheer thirty feet to the lower part of the trail. On the edge of the cliff stood a large willow tree, with long limp branches hanging down. As the first shower of stones clattered on the rock behind him, he was already leaping for one of the willow branches. He rode it half way down the cliff as it gave beneath his weight; he let go, falling down the other half to land in a tumble on the ground. Standing up, he looked back to the ravine, dusted himself off, and smiled. For the first time since this ordeal had begun, some understanding was coming, and even his bruises seemed worthwhile.

Still, the work intensified. Ioin carefully fashioned for himself a blunt ended spear, preparing yet another confrontation. He found Merlin later that day on the trail that circled the lake. When Merlin saw the spear, his mind told him this was carrying things too far, but his body was already preparing to meet the cast. Ioin threw it at his chest. Just before the moment of impact he turned so that the spear glanced off his forearm. This time nothing followed. Ioin came up to him and put his hands on his shoulders. "Good! Good!" he said, smiling and nodding his head.

Ioin was not through. He carved a dull wooden sword from the fallen limb of a nearby oak. He followed Merlin more closely than ever. Just when Merlin had settled

into some activity, Ioin appeared to strike or jab at him with his sword. Merlin soon grew adept in warding off every possible kind of blow. His courage and self-confidence increased; his body became strong and agile, and his senses sharpened.

It was later in the fall that Ioin finally considered the work nearly completed. He spent the next week digging some plants that Merlin did not recognize. He worked carefully and methodically, returning to the cave occasionally to consult one of his books.

The air was growing cooler each day, the wind more brisk. Autumn colors once again graced the trees.

Merlin sensed his time here was almost over. The next dawn, Ioin came to him and handed him a pouch containing a dark brown powder.

"It is your time Merlin. You know the rite," Ioin said.

Merlin was surprised at first; then nodded. Ioin looked deeply into his eyes, searching to see if he had done his teaching well.

"Remember, some have died in search of the vision. Your life will depend upon everything you do from the time you leave here until the time the medicine has been taken. After that, you need only be faithful to the guide that will come to you. Do you understand?"

Merlin nodded again.

"But do not fear. The boundaries of the living and the dead are not as commonly seen. For many live their lives never having been born, and many die before their bodies return to the earth. Some live with such vital power that they are invisible to the shadow lives, and their voices are heard even after they are laid in the ground. Some die for a time, to awaken again, and some are born for a time, to fall again into death."

A sadness welled up inside Merlin, but also a growing courage. He looked into Ioin's eyes.. They embraced each other. "I will miss you, Ioin," he said, knowing he

would never see him again. "I have yet to discover all that you have taught me."

"There is another legend, Merlin, concerning this lake. It is said that whoever can find the source of the waters of Llwyn Cerrig Bach will find the ancient Druidic treasures of Anglesey, and the sword of Macsen Wledig…Courage, and good faith Merlin."

"Good faith, Ioin."

He set out on the northern trail, the pouch tied to his belt.

The sky was clear blue over the peaks.

He looked up the steep forested slope to the east, letting his eyes follow the few furrows and ridges that might serve as possible routes of ascent. Towards the top, the trees fell away, leaving a series of high rock faces.

He pulled tight the shoulder straps he had made for his bag. A few hundred yards in, the forest grew thicker, and he pushed the low tree branches and underbrush to one side as he passed.

He walked on steadily with the branches tangling in his arms and legs, catching against his bag, forcing him to twist and crouch to free himself. The slope grew steeper. He cut a diagonal path across it, digging the inward edge of his feet into the soil, and passing along branch to branch so as to not be thrown downward.

The slope grew into a near cliff as he searched for an ascending ledge to climb, and found one. He pressed his body flat against the earth and stone. The route separated into two possible directions. He followed one, and was led to an unclimbable rock face. He retraced his steps, letting himself back down ledge to ledge on his belly, his feet dangling. He followed the other path upward, and found an opening where a few footholds and branches allowed him to let himself up through a long gully in the rock.

Stopping for a moment, he breathed the clear air, and looked down into the valley he was leaving. Far below, a narrow river wound its way into the lake.

He began again to lift his legs up the hill, feeling the first signs of weariness. He pushed himself for hours through the trees and bushes, pulling and clawing at the rocks and soil. He blessed the ground when it opened clear for a few yards; in these few easy steps he renewed his strength, and rested.

The slope grew yet steeper. He crawled on his hands and knees. He thanked the mountain when the soil was soft enough for him to kick his feet into it, and walk a few steps standing. He fought the fatigue that tried to overcome him. His legs, lifting, no longer moved one after the other. He directed each step, willed it, pushing his palm down on the top of his thigh to raise his body over his leg. He stepped up onto a rotten log, grabbed hold of a tree branch, wavered. He lost his balance, regained it. He wanted to collapse, thinking he could not go on, but knowing he must. He forced his legs to move.

Two days before leaving, under Ioin's direction, he had begun a fast; no food nourished him now. He called forth his sustenance from his own flesh. He drew deep breaths, taking the air as his food, until at last he heard the sound of pouring water. He followed it, sliding down into a gully the small stream had cut into the rock, leaning his body forward against the steep rocks where it cascaded. With his hands he held himself from falling fully into it, and sucked the water into his throat. He stood, feeling the water become the water of his flesh, climbing from the gully to begin the ascent once again.

He came to an open ledge, and looked down into the valley. The lake and the river appeared yet smaller. He watched the sun over the opposite ridge, wondering how much daylight was left.

He walked on, legs turned to stone, pulling himself forward with arms on branches. He moved into the rhythm of the climb; all else left him. He had neither the will nor the ability to think. He felt legs lifting, digging, edging into the slants of the soil, and arms pulling. Breathing, another step, another step, another step.

Again he felt he could not go on; again he wanted to collapse. There was not even enough flat ground on which to lie.

He climbed. He came to a small hollow where the roots of a huge oak had held the ground from falling, and let himself fall down into it for a moment's rest. Images came; he drifted toward a sleep of exhaustion. His eyes closed as his body sank and vanished into itself, falling toward a deep sleep...

"Merlin!" he heard. Who called? He opened his eyes, knew he must get to the top, knew he must not be caught on the side of the mountain when darkness came. He peered up the slope, trying to catch a glimpse of light on a ridge, hoping this would be where the land would again become flat, and he would be at the top. He climbed until he broke the crest of the ridge. Another ridge rose up behind it.

Again and again he climbed long and hard to break a ridge, hoping to give himself up to his exhaustion, only to find the land rising upward to yet another ridge.

What had seemed to be a climbable peak from far below now seemed to be an unending ascent. But he would continue, even until the utmost reserves of his will could not move him an inch further up the slope.

At last the steepness softened so he could stand, and the trees grew smaller.

He passed through a grove of oaks and elms. He blessed the trees for holding back the undergrowth, for the easier climbing that gave him the will to go on.

He rested frequently. Each time he stopped, his strength was renewed for the first few continuing steps, but each time the weariness followed more closely after. The mountain rose up steeper into jags and faces of stone. He inched his body upward, searching for footholds, balancing on fingertips pressed into tiny shallow lips of rock. He held close to the rock, embraced it with his arms and legs.

A vista opened; he looked across to the other mountains surrounding the valley. Soon he would be able to see beyond them. He climbed – pushed, crawled, stumbled upward. The land fell back a little, letting him off his knees onto his feet, letting him stand, not upright, but leaning forward. The land was merciful.

He climbed, rising upward as if nourished by his breath alone. He came to a huge stone hill protruding outward, making the slope still steeper. He put his hands and feet to it, accepted it, allowed the earth its ways knowing there was little left of him now, knowing he might die. He crawled on his belly to its crest.

Ahead, he saw the unattainable peak, still rising. But now he could see its summit, where its life communed with the sky; this was gift enough. He sat on top of the stone hill. For miles around he could see peaks surrounding him in a great circle. Over the western ridges, the land traveled flat for many miles to finally rise into another great range of mountains. The sun was setting over them, hovering in redness.

The wind swept over his sweating body. The land fell all around him in cliffs of immeasurable depth. He had no thoughts, felt not even contentment; he was here – that was all.

He took the pouch from his belt and opened it, emptying the powder into the palm of his left hand. He gathered the spit from his mouth with his tongue, and then put it on his fingertips. He mixed it with the powder

to form a few small pebbles. They would be part of his journey as well.

He listened to the sky and the wind, and looked over to the horizon. He ate them one after the other, as he fell into a deep inner silence, waiting, praying.

At first there was sickness, but it soon passed. Then it came for him.

It trembled; it did not speak. It beheld, not describing; it remained, not descending; it encompassed, not embracing. It reflected, it shattered. It loved – it made all die.

There was no struggle; the mountain had taken his will.

Now the wind came for what remained, and the wind was as alive as he, and his will was nothing against the elements.

If the wind were to sweep him down into the cliffs, he would not resist; if it were to bring rain and cold to freeze him to the stone, he would not protest. It would not be thwarted.

Yet, another voice struggled to speak, a small human voice, the voice of order, of human survival and will.

He threw his arms around himself and began to shiver. He stood, barely maintaining his balance, and began to walk back to the grove, seeking rest and shelter.

But the wind laughed at him, blew across the back of his legs, mocking him, calling him coward. He turned to confront it, and it vanished.

He began to push his way through more of the wiry bushes he had struggled with all day.

Here intrusion would not be tolerated, for the mountain was the sacred retreat of the earth. Here, she communed with herself; in peace, she knew and felt her own life, felt herself on her own great journey. For she needed, as all life needed, a place to be with herself alone.

He had not so respected her, and now bemoaned his forgetfulness.

The Mother knew her children's ignorance, knew in her wisdom they were destined to bring all her creatures harm and sorrow. And in this one tree, was the life of all trees, and it suffered for the woods laid waste to build ships of war.

He stumbled down through the trees.

The slopes were running in blood, dark red tides rippling downward.

The wind blew harder; darkness was coming on.

Why struggle? Why pit his will against the cold? It offered a soothing and eternal peace. Why not join the divine perfection, give up his mind and body and soul to the elements in their primal harmony?

But some deep instinct within him remained. When the freezing rain began to fall, he began to gather wood. He built a fire, chipping sparks with flint against his knife blade, catching an ember to a piece of charred cloth. The flames grew bright.

Run to comfort, fear the dark?

Not love the cold?

Will not discover the night?

He drew closer to the warmth of the flames. The wood was given. Was it given? Is this not for us, Mother? Then how shall we receive? In worship? No. But you are the giver. No...it is your love for us! You ask only that love be received, to know your love that we may more fully share in it.

And you are with me, inside of me, and I am inside you.

He laid a few more sticks on the fire.

It was not for him to choose. He did not choose. Gateways reveal themselves only to those who have labored long and hard, and in humility. They are not approached, but themselves approach.

He lay back on the ground and fell toward sleep. In the middle of the night he awoke, the wind whipping above

him in great gales. And he laughed, because it was good, and he had been heard.

He opened his eyes to the grayness of dawn, his ears to the spattering and dripping of rain, and the wind still shaking the treetops. For an instant he considered staying on the mountain, but no, he would return, and stronger. He prepared himself for the descent, the long fall.

He would return to the foot of the mountain, and there offer himself. The rain was coming; the wind blew harder. He began walking down the ridge, to find an opening in the underbrush. He found a steep chute, and squatted to slide down it on his feet, holding onto the branches as they swung downward with him. At the end of the slide he caught his feet on root clusters to break his fall, and hung on to the branches until the full weight of his body pulled against his arms, jerking him to a stop.

With every step it seemed he might tumble forward into the abyss. He angled across the less steep slopes, slid down others. He went down, deeper and deeper. He descended for hours, and still the land fell away. His clothes were soaked through by the rain; only his movement kept him warm. He must not stop.

He crossed ledges, balancing on the smallest accumulations of soil. Lurching across for handholds, his feet fell from underneath him, pushing stones and soil over the cliff's edge. He heard the stones bouncing again and again down the rock wall before crashing into the slope far below.

The soil grew deeper; he sunk his heels into it for better footholds. The rain ran down in tiny tricklings over the moss covered rocks. He struggled through the thick underbrush, trapped at times between branches, forced to crawl in the mud under fallen trees. He heard a stream, glimpsed up through the trees to see white water pouring over open rocks. He cautiously slid down into its

gully of smooth worn stone, and put his whole head forward into the running water. Then he drank, remembering, thanking.

Far below, the stream fell in a series of small cliffs. The land rose up high on either side of it as it fell deep into the earth. He knew he would not be able to leave the ravine once he had descended into it, but still he chose to remain with the stream.

He jumped in long strides down the gravel-covered gully, sliding in long steps, balancing. With his arms he lowered himself down between rocks, and slid over huge boulders to come crashing to their bottoms. He waded in the cold rushing water, crossing back and forth to find the downward path as one side and then the other blocked his passage. He rolled over huge logs on his belly while the stream rushed over him, drenching him.

With the stones and water he fell downward. The water poured, crashing, rushing on. His legs found steps, ridges, ledges; he descended. His legs grew heavy; the cold water ran over his ankles, and rain was on him, was all around him. He balanced on stones in midstream, straddled logs as he pushed and lifted himself along them.

The stream turned behind a ridge. He wondered if he had at last come to an impassable cliff. But it opened for him. He continued, fell, stumbled, slid, and the rocks fell, fell for hours beneath him, but he could not stop. The wetness would instantly chill him, stiffening his muscles. He denied his fatigue, as the land rose higher and higher above him on either side of the ravine.

His breath was clear and strong. Each step grew more cautious on the loose rocks of the stream bed, for he no longer had the strength to recover his balance should he lose it. The stream descended like a staircase, lower and deeper, and he caught a glimpse of the lake far below.

He walked for hours in the cold rain and rushing stream, over the hard and slippery rocks.

At last the stream leveled into a gentle slope. He walked fully upright, over fields of stone where the stream had washed wide. The stream crossed the trail above the lake. He was down.

He felt the soreness in his limbs, the cuts and scratches on his hands, his bruised body and aching muscles. The weight of his wet clothes dragged upon him, as he walked in utter exhaustion, and chills possessed him. But he was full, and thankful for his vision.

The Water to Land's End

he morning came damp, no life stirring. But now and then the cawing of a crow came forth from the gray fog. Above, gray clouds moved against a gray sky. Closer now, the fingered wings of he crow rose up from the ground to fly across the field, and disappear again into the mist. A slight wind lifted the undersides of the leaves of a lone-standing oak.

The brooch Ioin had given him was still fastened to the inside of his cloak. His steps were slow and hard, his legs fell one after the other as he wondered of the journey ahead. He caught himself. Ioin had once said, `there is a way of listening to the rhythm of your steps that will carry you most safely and surely to your heart's destination.'

He slowed his pace, and quieted himself. He moved through the slow swirling fog, feeling the passage of morning air in each of his breaths. He traveled to the north, leaving the valley.

But now his steps slowed; his own silence possessed him. Something is wrong. What? What do I feel? Only my imagination? It must be.

He tried to turn his mind to the trees and ferns, but even the woods seemed foreboding, draped in red and yellow pine needles.

The tree trunks stood stiff in the mists of morning – a cave of silence.

But maybe someone is calling? Who? Who? Branwen? Branwen, is all well with you? What is it? He tried to reach out to her, to touch her, listening for some response. Branwen!? But he could not know for certain. But he must.

He turned to the south and quickened his pace.

After several minutes he stopped. What is it I do? He felt the wind on his face, heard the birds, looked again

into the shadows of the tree branches. Nothing, just sights and sounds, no peace to be found; the unease was still growing inside him.

Again he began his impulsive striding, against the current of his own reason. He wanted to calm himself, but inwardly, beyond all sense, he was raging. No! No! What kind of madness is this? Am I possessed? He stopped again, breathing heavily. I must be calm.

He forced himself to see the green moss, the fallen leaves, the saplings in their delicate patterns of branches. He felt his breath, and for a moment was still, and from the silence the calling came again, stronger, clearer. He would go on.

A terrible loneliness overcame him, severing him from all human touching, from his own body. Strength, where to reach for strength? When he had sat with Ioin by the lake, looking at each other's reflection – what was it he said? Images, dreams, thoughts are not apart from the real world.

The forest opened into a great half-circle of sere and yellow fern, surrounded by trees hundreds of yards distant. The wind was blowing in waves over the ferns, from one end of the field to the other. There was something here, something unusual and powerful, not dangerous, but distant, strange. A sparrow hopped from bush to bush in front of him. The sky over the field was empty. Birds flew at the edge of the forest, not daring to venture into the open. The silence here was not empty, but he could not remain.

He hastened on. The air was lighter now, the trees not as thick.

Ioin spoke to him, in words he had heard once before ...in your belly is your balance, your quickness of movement and response; this is your tie to the world around you. In your heart is the power to see, to embrace your world and know danger before it draws near. In

your voice is the power to unite with the forces around you. Between your eyes, collect yourself, and know the absolute courage. By your crown, join in sacred communion with all life.

The village! Something is wrong. It is no peaceful calling. He searched his feelings, to be certain it was not only his fear of leaving something he loved

Twilight came; the forest grew dark. He no longer tried to avoid the puddles of rain, but splashed through them, holding his arms in front of his face as protection against the branches. Soon the air around him grew black. He could no longer see, and thought he must stop. But the moon came up, shining on the wet ground, casting the trees into outline. He walked late into the night, finally falling into exhaustion.

He woke up shivering, knew he must start to move. Another day passed, and night followed. He could no longer stand against his fatigue. He fell to the ground and rested for many hours; for how many he did not know.

It was late afternoon when he awoke. Lifting himself from the ground, he journeyed southward.

The trail turned around the side of a ridge, opening into a wide vista. He could see the familiar hills of the valley now, and his strength was renewed. He broke into a slow run, letting the gentle slope of the trail carry his weight down. He ran for almost an hour, and walked another two.

A smoky gray haze hovered over the valley. His fear rose again, and he began to run towards the last ridge that began the descent into the valley.

He came over the ridge, and stopped. His heart pounded in his chest; the blood raced in his temples. His hands clenched into fists. No! No! No! Why? He screamed in anger, charging down the mountain.

The fields were aflame; the hillsides were black. A line of flame and smoke advanced steadily across the yellow

pastures, spurred on by the wind.

He ran with all his speed down the hillside, to the outer edge of the village, and climbed over the earth-work fortification.

Nothing remained of the village center but circles of stone foundations, and piles of smoldering wood and straw. And the dead. Bodies lay strewn everywhere, some face down, others looking up in horror, arms and legs twisted, still feeling the fatal blows. The dead in pools of blood, gaping wounds in heads and chests. Headless, the heads were taken.

Branwen?! He ran to her home. The huts were hardly recognizable, but he found it. He stepped over Yetta's body to enter the chest-high circle of mud and stone of the outer walls. He threaded his way through the still burning wreckage of the collapsed roof, to Branwen's room. A large unburned portion of the roof had fallen over it. He took hold of a charred burning rafter and heaved it upward with all his strength. The roof section lifted and fell backwards. Not there. But he could feel her. She was alive. The well. He ran out, and found her.

She lay on the ground, on her back, wearing a torn cream-colored robe stained red on her right side. He approached. One of her hands stirred on the soil. He knelt down beside her on the grass, knowing she could not see him.

But by the faintest movements of her fingers, lips, and eyelids, he could tell she was listening to him. He need not speak to tell her he was with her now. He gently slipped his hands beneath her head and shoulders, and lifting her to his side, held her body to his with the cradle of his arms.

All his words had left him; only a hollow breathing came from his empty chest to swell his face and throat with a sadness that moved as some poison through all his mind and body. Her eyes half opened. It was her words,

in the lowest of whispers, that first came to join the stirring of the wind in the silence all around. He moved his hand between her hand and the ground, holding her fingers in his palm. She strained for a breath.

"Return with me in another life, return to me. Return with me. " Her fingertips traced the outlines of his nose, lips and eyes. "Merlin, do not mourn me...a time will come – I will try to remember."

He held his lips to hers, over her outgoing breath, and watched the light leave her eyes, as a shadow moved over her body, and stillness came.

"No, Branwen, no," he cried as her spirit departed. "I am with you now."

He lifted his eyes into the sky. The sun had dropped below the hills. Thc last part of orange on the clouds turned to gray.

His life emptied through his belly into the night. He held her tightly against the cold, and the darkness. Her last words became the night, became the blackest sky, the great expanse of a thousand stars.

The wind rose. He laid her gently down, and stood, and spoke to the night.

So perhaps now I will sleep with you, that we might awaken together. He drew his dagger from its sheath, and pressed its tip against the soft flesh below his breastbone. It tore through his tunic, opening his flesh into a trickling of blood. He looked into the night, saw the black sky through the wetness of his tears. His past, all his life with its memories and joys and sorrows, all vanished to leave him alone with the earth and the heavens, the wind and the knife. The wind swept up-ward, shaking the tree branches, awaiting his release. His fingers closed tightly around the dagger's grip. And he spoke, to the stars and the darkness.

"I will leave you. You will no longer lord over me. I will be free in a peace beyond your dominion." He held

the blade before his eyes, then lifted it high. It grew stronger in motion, flashing cold in the starlight. It moved in a slow arc against the glistening black sky, the wind stropping its edge, -- metal alive, ready to shriek in fury. He held it at arm's height, at the striking point.

The acrid smell of the still burning huts filled the air. The sky reflected in still pools of blood.

The power rose up in him. He gasped, and the dagger dropped to the ground.

No, even this cannot be granted me.

He shuddered, binding his sorrow by his will, joining it into a new resolve to find another way.

He stooped down, lifting her body with her long hair trailing, and walked up onto a grassy hill, near a pile of stones. He laid her down, picked up a small flat rock.

He began scraping the soil, scraping deeper and deeper, scooping the dirt out with his hands. But the ground was hard. It would be a shallow grave. He lifted her into it, and knelt beside her.

He spoke to her in his heart, now the only way he could.

"Gladly would I lay myself down there instead of you. Gladly would I lie by your side until the wind and rain covered us both in the earth's body. With joy would I let my life run into your eyes and breath and limbs, so that you were full, and I empty...so that my blood be the blood that serve your life. Your skin is cold, friend, so white. I cannot see the rise and fall of your chest, or the movement of your eyes beneath eyelids. It is a deep sleep, I think. And I cannot join you – but not because I would not choose it...I have much to do before this peace be granted me. It will not be long, and your sleep will hurry you on, while my few years pass. Yet not all my power can stir you, nor knowledge of the high arts bring you back. If my lips touching yours could return your breath, or my body warm your blood...but it seems my god will hear no appeals, and I but a mortal man who cannot bestow upon one so loved the gift of life."

Many moments passed as the wetness of soil and blood chilled his hands, and the night wrapped him in its cold. And it was long before he could bring himself to place her hands together over her breasts, to look for the last time at the wispy brown lashes of her soft eyelids, and the fading red of her smooth lips, before sweeping the piled soil back over her feet and legs, belly and breast. As he pushed moist earth over the silent face, his breath broke into sobbing, and he had to turn his eyes away.

He could no longer cry. But a wail rose up inside him, the wail of an animal that could not comprehend death, could no longer allow it to be. He fell face down over her grave, lying there for hours until at last sleep came.

He awoke just before dawn. It was bitterly cold now, and the wind blew fiercely over the hill that glowed in the color of hot iron. Dew and damp air had drenched his clothing. Shivering, he set out to the west, to the sea.

He walked over bodies, not seeing. He passed the lakeshore. Water lapping against stone. In the water, the body of a child floating, face down. He waded out to it, turned it over. In the dawn light he could still make out the features of the puffed face. It was Kendall. He carried him onto the lakeshore and laid him down, then gathered flat stones as the sky lightened into gray. He laid them over the body, placing the last stones over the face, and walked on.

He followed the river out of the valley, winding down toward the sea. He pulled berries from bushes as he walked, stuffing them into his mouth. The path led him into twilight, onto cliffs high above the ocean's crashing. As he stood, watching the gray clouds mingling with the last red light of day on the flat horizon, a voice came.

It was his own voice, words that had been growing in his belly, words he could not let himself hear. But now

they pushed upward to his throat, and called forth the unadmitted tears. In a hoarse whisper he said to the sea and to the clouds and to all he saw, "I do protest your cruelty." Now at last they had been spoken, and in a broken voice he said again, "I do protest your cruelty." The violence and the sadness erupted within him, as with all his breath and strength he threw his voice against the incoming wind. "Why?!"

He clenched his fists at his sides. He stumbled back to a ledge protected from the wind, falling down behind it. He looked into the sky; the coming night would be black and churning. It began to rain.

His sole companions were a bitter wind, a blowing mist, and a starless darkness. Everywhere was the wind, ceaseless; everywhere was the water, unrelenting rain. No warm thought could penetrate a night like this, to reach out like a distant beacon on a black stormy sea. He struggled to hold her image, to see her face, but the wind dispersed his every effort. Below, the waves hammered on the shore, and the gulls searched in strident cries.

He pulled his knees tightly into his chest, and slept. Streaks of light blue in the sky heralded the coming day. He sat up; the wind was dry on his face, the smell of brine strong. He stood up to look out over the horizon. As his eyes traveled over the blue and black glimmering pools on the water's surface, some movement caught his eyes. The huge glistening gray backs of a herd of whales rode in long graceful arcs through the water. And something more! His gaze traveled down the high mast, to the sail furled and tied to the crossbeam. Overcome by his desire to be released from his sorrow, he began to run towards the cliff edge, threading his way down toward the ship, through long gullies broken into the steep hills on the shore. Stones and loose dirt spilled ahead of him.

On the deck, voices shouted in haste and fear.

The anchor was hauled in, the sail made ready. The captain was not now concerned with the lone figure scrambling down the hillside; he watched for signs of movement on the plateau above. A man of huge physique, young and square-shouldered, stood on the shore at the ship's bow, holding a knife.

Merlin reached the shore. He finally realized the panic he had caused, but continued to approach. The sun glared in his eyes. The captain still watched the cliffs, expecting any moment to see coils of rope sailing over them, and warriors following.

"I am alone, I –" He hardly saw the pounding fist that met his jaw; his ordeal had left him with neither the strength nor the will to fight. The man picked up his limp body and carried him onto the ship. They set sail.

After a few minutes he came to. A band of sailors stood over him, in a hazy outline, speaking a strange language. His half-sleep was broken by a bucket of cold seawater. He gasped, and shook his head. The sailors laughed. He spat out the brine, and looked at the faces above him. The man who had hit him reached down and helped him to put himself on his feet.

"Welcome to the Cadwgawn," he said with a big smile. "I am called Dannick." He spoke in Merlin's tongue.

"Then I should call you Dannick Strong Arm," Merlin replied, rubbing his swollen jaw. "On a better day I would not let a blow like that go by."

"Better let them go by," Dannick joked, "than stop them the way you did!"

The sailors gave another boisterous laugh, all relieved to see Merlin was alone, and no attack coming.

"But you must know, a trading vessel does not long remain with its original owners once they begin to trust the coastal *cenedl* of these parts," he added.

Merlin could not help being lifted by the spirits of the men, even though mention of the coastal bands stirred his sadness and anger.

"Well, to work, we have a ship to sail," said one.

"And a port to make," added another.

"And mead and young lassies," a third chipped in.

The men patted Merlin on the back and left. But Dannick watched the expressions on Merlin's face, and guessed that something was wrong. When the others had dispersed, he brought Merlin to a bench and sat him down. He left, but returned shortly with crusty bread and dried beef.

"Eat some of this now."

Merlin shook his head; his stomach had not held food for several days now, and he was still too upset to swallow. Dannick left the food beside him on the bench, then returned to his post near the rear of the ship. Merlin sat, growing sick with the pitching and rolling of the deck.

All around him he saw nothing; his ears heard only a death-like silence. There was no hope of peace. He felt paralyzed, unable to move himself from the suffocating embrace of his own pain.

Morning and afternoon passed. Night came. Dannick brought him a thick blanket, and he slept heavily.

Not long after dawn they reached land, sailing a westward course across St. Georges Channel. They disembarked, leaving the ship well guarded, and traveled on to Rathfarnham and the mountains of Kildare.

The next morning they arrived in the village. There was a great commotion about, and they were hardly noticed. Finally the captain took hold of the arm of a young boy, and asked in another dialect, "What be the cause of all this excitement?" The villagers poured past on all sides, running toward the southern part of the village. Voices

carried loud, angry, and chaotic over the growing human stream.

The boy looked up to the captain, opening his eyes wide. He smiled with closed lips. "It is The Clearing."

The captain let him go, and stepped back. "My God," he muttered to himself, "never in all my life... " It was true then. They were not just stories. The other sailors crowded around, wanting to know what had happened, but he only said over and over, "The Clearing, The Clearing." He joined the mass of people walking to the south, his men and Merlin following.

The crowd massed around a single hut. The captain pointed. "The accuser. This is the tribal court, the law of this *tuath*. All gathered here are the witnesses. God himself is the judge."

The crowd suddenly grew silent. The accused approached, walking wrapped in a white sheet, bearing a skull in his hand. The crowd parted to let him through. He kneeled down before the house of his accuser, made the sign of the cross, and kissed the skull. For a long time he prayed silently. The villagers watched on in awe and dread of the imminent visitation of the Almighty. The accuser came forth, pale and trembling. He took his place in front of the kneeling man, and held his palm upright. "In fear of your life before the wrath of God, I command you now to speak the truth."

The accused responded. "If I should lie, as all here are my witness, may this man's sins," he began, holding up the skull, "be laid upon my soul, and all the sins of his forefathers back to Adam. May the just punishment for their evil, their weakness and their sorrow, rest upon my soul now and to come evermore."

Some turned their heads in fear and sorrow; others looked on more intently. "But if you, my accuser, have spoken falsely, and from the evil in your heart, then

may this curse be yours, and your soul made to perish everlastingly!"

The silence of the crowd broke in a wave of whispers and gasps. Only the village elders had ever before heard the curse spoken. Often a generation passed without The Clearing. Most chose to suffer wrong, rather than force even the worst of offenders to undergo such an ordeal.

Now came the time of waiting. The people sat down on the ground and grew quiet again. They watched the sky, and listened for the wind. The trial ended at nightfall. If by that time nothing had befallen the accused, and no omen had been given, he would be pronounced innocent by the people. No word would ever again be spoken against him. But from that time on, the accuser would be looked upon with fear and mistrust.

The sun grew toward noon. The wind began blowing up black clouds from behind the horizon.

The captain whispered to his men. "There will be no trading here for days. Let us go on through Kildare."

They departed, heading toward a range of black and green mountains. The road rose swiftly beneath them as they walked, and by the end of the day they had reached the first of the ridges they were to cross. The land opened up before them, rolling hills of orange black sod locked within the rings of higher peaks. The evening mists had just begun their slow churning down the high hillsides, with the low sun setting them aglow from within. They rounded another hill. Merlin stopped.

He was looking toward a plateau several hundred yards to the north. "What are they?"

"Nothing. Just the ringstones," a man answered.

"Ringstones?" The name sounded familiar, but why? Ringstones! Ioin's story! That was it! He rushed across the soggy turf.

"No!" The captain's voice trailed after him.

The captain turned to his men. "Nightfall approaches;

we cannot wait." It was more than ordinary danger that he feared; the tales of strange sightings and unearthly deaths in these hills were too numerous to count. His men did not argue; they hastened on down the trail.

But after a moment, Dannick stopped. He strained his eyes to see across the plateau, but Merlin was nowhere to be seen. He started to walk again, but something would not let him rejoin the group. He turned and headed back up the trail, searching for the place he had last seen Merlin. When he found it he sat down and began to wait while twilight fell around him.

Merlin drew closer to the rings of the huge standing stones, ancient and silent watchers. Though ever communing with the moon and stars, they came alive but a few hours of the year – when the earth passed into the moon's shadow, when the sun found the center of the sky and knew the passage of the seasons, when the great north star marked the earth's place in the heavens, then would these stones draw breath, and pulse, and feel the wetness of the dew upon them.

He reached out to touch one; his fingertips ran over rough stone. Giant of another race, your shadow falls upon a hundred men, through a hundred generations.

Twilight shadows lengthened at the feet of towering gray blocks, interspersed between bands of copper light. Two score stones stood in two great con-centric circles, the larger on the outside. Huge slabs of rock lay horizontally across their tops. The Giant's Dance!

He dared to enter. The moon rose, casting a yellow light over all. He walked through the outer ring, listening, approached the inner ring, passed through. In the center was an altar. He was trembling now, not with fright, but because something was here.

The winds on the distant hills spoke in a low wail as he stepped toward the altar. Life. His own. He was still alive, even having lost her. And his life would create, and would

bring forth, and would make the world anew.

The clouds that had been gathering all day now rose into a black tower overhead. There was an inscription on the altar stone. Deep rumblings stirred from the clouds. The wind gusted. A bolt of lightning cracked open the sky. He deciphered the ancient tongue. Lightning struck inside the inner circle, for an instant set the inscription aglow. He looked over to the grass burned black, still flaming, and knew. The air exploded in fire and crashing all around him as thick sheets of rain drenched his clothing. He knew the very power of the elements themselves would serve his undertaking, bound as they were by the power of an ancient priesthood.

And he took hold of the darkness, saying, "Your circle may well offer guidance to the farmer, but one day these stones will yield a greater harvest not of this earth alone."

Dannick still waited, and although he grew fearful in the darkness, he could not leave. When the storm came he tried to take shelter under a large shrub.

At last Dannick heard footsteps in the darkness.

"Merlin?" Dannick said.

"I am here," Merlin answered.

"What has happened?" Dannick asked.

"Nothing," Merlin replied. "The stones speak."

The strikes of lightning illuminated Dannick's huge form crouching underneath the shrub, just shaking his head. Merlin was amused. "The rain seeks out those who would not befriend it of their own accord," he said, holding his upturned palms to the sky," Merlin preached.

"Why God gave to us the likes of you..." Dannick jested.

"Come, let us go," Merlin beckoned.

"It is raining!" Dannick protested.

"Yes, everywhere," Merlin confirmed.

"What 'ave you done now?" Dannick asked, half joking, and adding "Come on, we will have to run the next few miles..."

They caught up to the main group, who had made a shelter of oiled skins. They spent the night huddled under blankets, waiting for the night to clear. And Merlin thought about all that had happened.

In the morning he was awakened by voices conversing in excited tones. It was the captain, and another man who was sweating and nearly naked. Merlin recognized the runner the captain had hired at Rathfarnham to bring back news from the inland.

The captain shouted over his sleeping men, "Everyone up! We are put on the run. We must return to the Cadgawn."

"What danger?" Merlin asked.

"The *ri ruirech* of the eastern land is displeased with one of the coastal kings, and if you value your head you will not be wasting time with more foolish questions."

They began a forced march to the sea, arrived at the ship in two days, and set sail. As the land grew distant, they watched the gathering of mounted warriors with long spears and horned helmets that filled the coast.

The days wore on. Merlin, no longer absorbed in the excitement of the strange land, again grew deeper into depression. Once again his own death loomed closer.

He stood on the outer edge of the deck, overlooking the waves, feeling the coldness of his tears on his cheeks, warm at first, then cooled by the wind.

He heard the call of a gull high overhead, and the soft lapping of the waves on the ship's sides.

It began to rain. The salty drops ran down his face, over his eyelids, his cheeks and lips. She was gentle, and did love you. Why send her forth into such a life? And where would you now take me? I am young, but not as young as she; her faith was in you. But as for me, now you must earn my love, where once I would have given it freely. You must prove the wisdom of your will over mine, where once I would have served you.

He watched the rain fall in sheets before him. He realized he had not seen the sun for days; it lay buried beneath layers of thick gray clouds. The boat rode the waves high upon the crests, down into the troughs, again and again, and the water splashed. The light dimmed behind the clouds.

Nor will you have my despair, though my strength be but a grain of sand upon all your shores...till it is my strength. Somewhere I will find hope, though I no longer know what that means. When it comes, I will be ready. Perhaps a voice from the waves, calling me to their peace. Or a summons from the wind to join its eternal flight. What need have I of this body?

The face of Branwen appeared to him, in her dying moment. He let his head and shoulders hang over the ship's railing. He wept and his body shook, and his breath was lost to sobbing.

He felt an arm around his shoulders. He raised his head.

Neither he nor Dannick said anything for a long time, but for a moment they held each other's eyes, and Merlin was warmed from the surrounding cold.

But still he was alone with his sorrow, and his aloneness seemed forever.

The night winds began to blow harder across the deck; Dannick threw a blanket around Merlin's shoulders.

High in the clouds the wind churned, opening a small patch of black sky. A few dim stars shined through, before vanishing again behind the moving gray clouds.

Dannick spoke. "There is a fire in the hut. Come warm yourself."

Merlin heard him, but at first did not want to move. Then finally he followed after Dannick to the hut.

The next day Merlin learned from the captain that he was to

be left off at the next port. He considered the captain's decision, but kept his own counsel.

In the afternoon they were rounding Land's End.

Merlin looked to the sea of white crashing, and to the high plateaus of green grass dropping in stony cliffs down to the shore.

He raised his voice above the wind and roaring breakers.

"Hoist sail! Hoist sail!"

The captain ran over to him, unable to believe his own ears. "What are you shouting about? Ordering about my men on my ship?"

"I wish to make land here," Merlin announced.

"What?" the captain asked, incredulous.

"This is where I will make land," Merlin repeated, as though not hearing the captain's protests.

"You are mad. I cannot take my ship into those waters," the captain replied.

Dannick and a couple of crewmen had come to listen.

"Then I will take a small boat," Merlin countered, undeterred.

"Those are lifeboats, and are needed on the ship. And it is much too dangerous as well."

Merlin would hear no protest. This was the shore he wanted. It was from here he would venture forth.

He looked up to the other men.

"I will take you, Merlin." It was Dannick.

Merlin knew he understood, where others could see only foolishness. They shared a deep smile.

"I will not lose a good crewman," said the captain, making one last protest.

"But captain, who will return the boat?" asked Dannick.

"That's right. Someone will have to...wait a minute."

The crewmen laughed. The captain met Merlin's eyes. "All right, but watch those rocks," he said to Dannick, who was already putting the boat down on the leeward side, where the waves were lower. Then he turned to Merlin.

"Listen carefully Merlin. Once we leave the side of the Cadwgawn, we will be only a branch on the waves. Whatever happens we must keep the bow moving straight through them, or we will roll before we know what hit us."

Each pulled an oar. Thirty yards from the ship, the waves grew huge again, lifting them high and forward, dropping them deep into troughs. They traveled swiftly, pulling the oars with all their strength. They soon tired, but the shore grew closer as they headed for a small patch of sand at the cliff base, until the boat grounded in two feet of water.

"Run in with a wave," Dannick shouted, "or you will be pulled under."

Merlin watched the swift and steep undertow, chose his moment, and jumped. His feet slipped on smooth rock, and he went under, and came back up coughing. Barely able to stand in the swirling waters, he pushed his legs a few steps forward. The undertow caught him, threw him back, but he remained standing. He waded ahead, seeking out footholds on the rock slope beneath him. Again he slipped. He crawled the last ten feet to the shore as the waves washed over him, and collapsed, his face into the sand, hearing the sound of his breath against the wind and waves.

He remembered Dannick. He looked up to see him struggling against the churning waves, as the small boat was carried out on the jetties.

Merlin lifted himself from the sand, saw the tide was coming in.

Within an hour this small bit of shore would be covered beneath tons of seawater. Only ten or twelve feet from the water's edge the land rose in stone cliffs hundreds of feet high.

He searched for a way up. Sixty feet or so above him a series of narrow ledges ran diagonally up across the rock face, but it was a sheer vertical wall to reach them.

He was exhausted; the cliff seemed unclimbable. He needed rest, but there was no time; the waves were already advancing on the beach. He had perhaps an hour to climb from the shore, but he could count on only half of that.

He would have to be so high that he could not be dragged down by the incoming waves breaking below him on the cliff, or lose his footing on the wetted stone.

Needing to gather his strength for the attempt, he lay on the beach halfway between the cliff and the high point of the water, thinking the waves might wake him should he fall asleep. Several times his eyelids fell; he shook himself. All sense of time escaped him.

He pushed a long stick into the sand a foot from the water's edge.

A huge breaker stormed high onto the beach, sending a thin sheet of water rushing to the cliff.

He must begin. He shook his arms and legs, rubbed his hands together, and studied the rock wall. The first step would be hard. He placed one foot in a small hollow about waist high. With his other foot he thrust upward, hoping to find a secure edge for his fingers in his second of forward balance before falling back.

There was nothing.

He needed to press his body upward and flat against the rock face, and shift his weight to the high foot.

Once more he set his foot upon the rock, and leaped upward against it with the other.

His hand wiped over it, searching for an edge, finding none. He fell back. He tried again, fell back again. His strength was diminishing; the waves swirled at his feet, the tide rising quickly. He examined the rock again. A

long crevice ran from the ground toward him on an upward diagonal, to a point just below the first of the ledges. During his training with Ioin he had learned how to use every muscle in his body to the best advantage; now it was necessary. He removed his leather sandals, tying them over the rope belt at his waist. He leaned his right side against the cliff, placed his right foot against the vertical edge provided by the crevice, and pushed both hands into it, one chest high, one above his head. He lay back against the cliff wall, then pushed up with his left foot, and pulled hard with his arms, trying to maintain a precarious and strained balance as he sought to secure his left foot against the vertical edge.

For a moment, he held, but then fell back. He moved his hands for better leverage, as the water splashed and surged over his calves.

He positioned himself again, drew a deep breath, and summoning all his strength, thrust upward. His left foot found the crevice. His full weight pulled against his arms as he pushed against the rock with his feet.

He was on the wall; he steadied himself, moving slowly. His fingers crept upward, moving his hands inch by inch, shuffling his feet forward in the crevice.

He climbed a foot, a yard, another yard. He worked his way up to the height of the crevice, and stretched his body upward, straining his arm to its utmost length. His fingertips trembled, a foot below the first ledge. His legs started to shake. He jumped. His hand clutched at the ledge, slipped. The other one held. He dangled on one arm, glimpsed the sea far below. Pulling hard, he unlocked his elbow, lifting himself high enough to secure his other hand, to pull himself up to his chin, to his shoulders, until his elbows rested on the ledge. Letting out long breaths, he rested.

He pulled up one knee; his fingers climbed upward on the flat wall as he placed his foot on the ledge. He pulled

up one knee; his fingers climbed upward on the flat wall as he placed his foot on the ledge.

He pushed himself upward flat against the rock, then stood. Looking over his shoulder, he saw Dannick still struggling in the waves. A huge wave lifted the boat, crashed down with it. It disappeared into a trough, returned.

He moved along the ledge until it opened wider into a staircase that let him scramble up the steep slope on all fours. The slope softened, the rock became more jagged, providing better holds, as he climbed the next hundred feet without difficulty. The waves crashed rocks below, shooting spray high onto the cliff.

He waited while his strength returned, and his breath slowed, before beginning the long but now sure ascent. He ran up the rows of ledges like an animal, jumping up one to another. The land fell back farther, losing its steepness. He climbed another hundred feet; soon he would reach the plateau. Upward, upward! He felt a power in himself that he had never known before. He roared, and laughed at the huge waves. He looked out over the sea; Dannick had reached the *Cadwgawn*. He ran up the last of the ledges.

Huge piles of black clouds rose up over the sky, and gusts of wind began to blow in gale force. The setting sun painted the clouds in fiery red, and the air grew icy cold.

Merlin stood on the plateau, as the wind battered him, until he could no longer hold his place against it. He strained to walk forward into it. The wind caught him in mid-step, threw him back. He turned sideways and stood still, leaning against its force, but every sixth or seventh gust threw him back, forcing him to replant his feet. For many, many moments he held his ground and listened,

and watched. The waves, white-crested hills, made thunder on the cliffs. This was the ocean's peace.

Land's End.

The place of dreams where land and water meet, where substance joins heart's vision.

He took his power as its own, giving voice to a new vision...

Now at last is the earth beneath my feet, and the ground ringing with my steps, for the miles of my life's journey are measured, and my roads marked in the wayposts of the wind. Land. I will make my peace with you. I will lay down with you and give you child. I will hear your voice, and not forsake you.

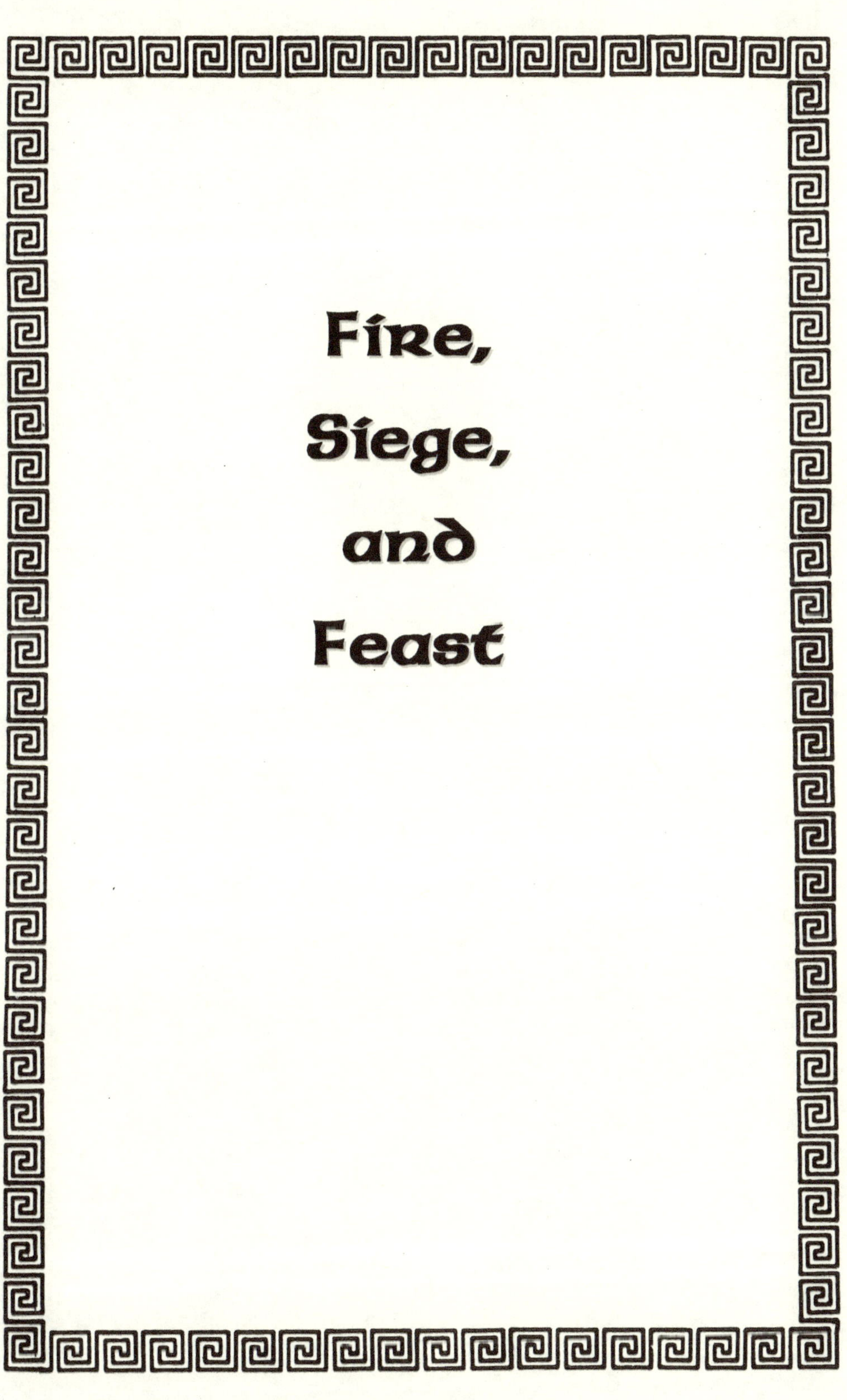

Fire, Siege, and Feast

s he dead?

"Yes, he is dead.

She dismounted without the help of her attendant, laid an ear to the chest. "No, he is not dead."

"Better leave him, your grace. Any more time here and the storm will find us too."

"No."

"Your grace, we are in danger of –

"Silence! Are you blind?"

"Your grace?"

"This boy is a Pendragon."

The men drew back.

"Fools, I say he is not dead. Lay him on my horse."

They did as they were commanded.

The troop turned inland, over the low coastal ridge.

"Branwen? Branwen?"

"How is his fever?"

"Still high."

"Has he opened his eyes yet?"

"Not for three days now."

"Keep him well bathed, and tell me if there is any change in his condition."

"Yes, your grace."

Merlin could hear the voices. He felt the cold autumn air was in his lungs. Outside, dry leaves crackled on wind blown branches. No birds were calling. The air was crisp, laden with the smells of rotting leaves, and the sea.

He was lying in a large bed, with blankets of wool and silk. His hands and feet were wrapped in warm wet cloths. The room was made of square logs laid one on top of the other, covered in hides.

By the hearth, a woman was bent over a cauldron. She pulled from it a few steaming rags, and came to him.

"So it seems you have beheld the face of death, young Pendragon. Or should I say, Prince Merlin?"

He opened his eyes upon the woman who stood beside his bed. She was slender, and of fair height. Beneath the veil of her headcloth, black hair hung down to her waist. Her eyes were green, and her skin like cream, her features fine.

"We can thank the Hooded Ones for your recovery," she said.

"Where am I?" he asked.

"In the fortress of King Gorlois."

"And you?"

" I am the Queen, Ygerne."

" I am indebted for your kindness, my lady."

"Rumors have spread of your wanderings. What brings you now to our coast?"

"A westerly wind, or the season," Merlin said simply.

"Well, then I will not keep you from your rest," she said and departed.

The coming night was the eve of Samhain. The grazing season was over, and the new year was to begin. All fires were put out, and then lighted again; the juncture of this world and the other world opened. The dead returned to roam with demons and unknown creatures, and the future could be seen.

"Prince Merlin, will you join us at the celebration tonight?" It was Ygerne's handmaiden.

"Yes, I would like that."

"It begins at moonrise in the main hall."

" I will be there," he said.

He looked for his clothes. A new set had been laid out for him, breeches and tunic of finely woven wool, and a blue cloak embroidered with garnets. He dressed and went to the hall.

Upon entering, he met the faces of bulls and stags and boars and all manner of beasts. The masks were well-crafted, and held expressions of terror and dread.

"Welcome, Prince Merlin," a strong voice said "King Gorlois?" Merlin turned toward him. He saw before him an old warrior, a king, courage and daring now having passed into wisdom. There seemed a kindness in his eyes.

Gorlois continued in measured tones. "There is something of a legend growing about you," he advised.

"Sire?" Merlin asked.

"Something about a cloaked figure appearing miraculously atop a high cliff, amidst thundering and the opening of the heavens." The King spoke with some amusement, but not without respect. It was commonly believed that the gods often took human form to explore their dominions. Disaster befell anyone who intended them harm and good fortune to those who helped them. The King continued, not really questioning Merlin's mortal nature, but cautiously exploring what manner of man he might be.

"The peasants are calling him Cyr Myrddin."

Merlin nodded. Ygerne drew closer, to hear his response.

"They do me too much honor," he answered.

The King smiled, but awaited further explanation.

"Yet a man is named by his deeds alone, and even a god would rather you know his work than his name. But I hope our god of sacred waters is not displeased."

This answer seemed to please the King for the time.

"Well, let us meet some of my men," the Kind said. They approached a man of curly brown hair and brown eyes, who smiled when they approached. "This is Brennan, captain of the guards, and a better man can not be found on all the western coast." Brennan nodded his head low, then turned to address Merlin.

"Prince Merlin, it was I who laid you on Queen

Ygerne's horse. Welcome to the kingdom."

"Then I owe you my thanks and my friendship, Brennan. Some day I hope to repay you."

They moved on through the swirling crowd.

The King reached for two full goblets of wine from a passing tray, and handed one to Merlin.

"Long life and our friendship, Merlin."

"Russ, over here." A tall thin lad of about seventeen years, with reddish brown hair falling over his eyes, walked over to them.

"Russ, this is Merlin who you have asked me about," then turning to Merlin, "Russ is my nephew."

Russ looked up to Merlin. "They say you have spent much time in the dark forests. Perhaps you would hunt with me on the morrow."

"Have we the favor of Cernunnos?"

"Always." Russ smiled, happy with the companionship.

"Before first light then," Merlin answered.

"Good." Russ returned to his escort, who was awaiting him anxiously.

" A fine lad he is; you will not be sorry for his company."

Merlin shook himself from his own thoughts. "Sire, please allow me to retire. It has been a long journey, and I would find my strength again."

"Of course," the King answered.

Merlin began walking down the long torch lit hallways. to his room. Ygerne followed him, walking swiftly to catch up to him. "Merlin."

Merlin turned and waited for her to draw closer.

"My Queen?"

Ygerne hesitated for a moment. "Do be careful on the morrow. I sense some ill tides in the wind."

Merlin met her eyes, fell in some sudden depth as for an

instant it seemed his destiny was intertwined with hers. Then he drew back again, as though struck by some power.

With her eyes, she questioned what he had seen. But it was gone, and he could not tell her.

But he offered, "To me the spirits of the forest are not strangers." Then with a nod he begged his leave, and returned to his room.

In the early part of morning he was awakened by a knock on his door, and a voice he had heard before. "Merlin, the stags await us." It was Russ.

He dressed, and they walked toward the outer gates.

"Russ, what weapons have you chosen for us?" Merlin asked.

"Spears. Do you want something else?"

"No, spears are good," Merlin answered.

"We will find them at the gate," Russ said.

As dawn broke they left the road, heading into the heart of the forest. The hooting of an owl passed through the silence. The branches, laden with dew, soaked their clothes as their footsteps fell upon the forest floor.

"Remember the girl that you saw me with last night?"

"Yes, the pretty one?" Merlin asked.

"That is Olwen. We are soon to be wedded."

The comment caught Merlin off guard. "So you will have sons?" he asked.

"Yes, and daughters as well. Olwen is young and strong."

Merlin paused. "I think I am no man's son, and will be no man's father."

"Have you not found a woman?"

"Yes, I have found her, and she is with me still," Merlin answered.

"With you still?" Russ asked.

Thirty feet across the grove stood six huge warriors, wearing horned helmets and draped in ragged fur. A spear came alive, shot forward in an explosion of muscle and savage cry, a dark streak in the air – it passed through Russ's

upper abdomen, throwing the body back, pinning it to an oak. The face twisted convulsively, the head slumped and hung limp, eyes and mouth open. The blood poured in spurts.

The warriors laughed.

Merlin threw his spear, piercing one's shoulder. Another spear shot toward him.

Clasping his hands together and locking his arms into a rigid wedge, he sidestepped and struck the spear down inches from his body. In one motion his cape was off and he was running in full stride, as another spear flew by him.

The warriors nodded approvingly of their quarry; this would make the hunt more rewarding. They set out in pursuit.

Merlin reached out farther with each step; the ground moved beneath him, trees and branches flying by, whipping his arms and legs.

He gulped the air, his chest heaving; his heart smashed against his chest.

He twisted his body around obstacles, jumping creeks and rocks, running over small hills. The weariness was growing in his legs, and he could still hear them not far behind. His breath heaving, he knew he could not long sustain the pace.

Were there more? Did they have horses?

The forest was not thick enough to lose them, but ahead, some mist was settling.

Pain and exhaustion filled his legs. The breath was gone from his voice. Footsteps crashed toward him. He hid. He hid deep within himself, and there he heard Ioin...a warrior must learn well the meaning of position and stance. On the battlefield, or in the feasting hall, he must know where to stand, where lies the place of greatest strength.

This is the true armor to wear always, an armor as fluid as the air, neither weighing you down nor blunting your instincts. It intensifies and focuses your every sense….He stood where no blow could touch him. He turned toward his attackers, and he found words from a distant place.

"I am Cyr Myrddin, and servant of the kingdom. Fear the wrath of the Way all you who would harm me!"

He spoke not to the men, but to the wind and the sun and the forest, and the silence within. Hoof beats grew on a distant road, coming closer, two, three, four, a dozen horses. He stood where he could escape death, knowing it was not his time, knowing he could not be harmed.

"MERLIN!"

God, it was Brennan. He let out his breath. The approaching steps turned, receded again into the blanketing mist.

He drew a long deep breath, and in an unsure voice called out, "Brennan, here!"

The ride back to the fortress was short. From the tower above the main gate, Queen Ygerne watched their return. The King greeted them below.

"And Russ?" The King asked.

"He is dead," Brennan answered.

"Did you not find the body?"

"There was not time, sire." Brennan answered. This was no roving band. We have been brought news the inland tribes are massing for war. I fear attack within a day's time."

"Then war it will be. See to our defenses. Merlin, come with me." The King led Merlin into his chambers.

"Did he die quickly?" The King asked.

"Fools."

"Sire?"

"We all are fools, not warriors. I now look back on battlefields of three decades. No more than fields of blood, no valor, no honor, nothing but blood. And more blood. My arm is yet strong, but now I would rather carry my sword into a different battle. All these years I have been struggling with an enemy I did not know was myself. And you, too, have the blood of a warrior, but perhaps you will someday see your foe in the bright shield drawn against you."

"I have only one life to avenge," Merlin spoke.

"And so it goes on forever. Do you think the tragedy of *Cae Gaer* has not been told by now? Do you think the travels of a Pendragon go without notice? It is known you were there. They are calling it the Valley of the Lost."

Merlin drew back, unwilling to feel that pain again for even a moment. "Is this what you brought me here for?"

"Hold fast to your courage, Merlin."

Merlin met his gaze, and felt naked in his sorrow. "There were hardly a dozen good swords amongst them."

"So always the innocent are slaughtered, while their executioners find honor in battle."

"Sire, I would speak no more of this," Merlin said.

King Gorlois nodded, and then began with a new question. "Prince Merlin, they say you have been trained in black arts of war?"

Merlin said nothing, but did not deny it.

"The enemy will come in great numbers. Come speak with me after our meal."

Merlin nodded his ascent, "Sire. And one question... how did Brennan come to be on the eastern road?"

"I thought you knew," the King said, "Ygerne sent him after you, fearing some danger."

Merlin nodded, and returned to his room, and bathed. Then he fell into a deep sleep...

The guards paced on the ramparts. No sign yet on the horizon. The sun reached high in the sky, began to fall low again. The peasants from the surrounding farms and villages were hurried into the fortress, as fortifications were strengthened, ditches dug deeper. Large stores of food and water were gathered, and the smiths labored to repair damaged weapons. Those with armor put it on.

Gorlois, too, walked the ramparts. And consulted with Brennan. "How much longer?"

"Until dawn. That and twilight are the times they hold most favorable to passage to the otherworlds." How long can we hold them out?"

"An hour at most," Brennan answered.

"Then we are ourselves not long for the otherworlds."

"It is true – but good faith, sire."

"Then good faith, Brennan."

The night was black, the sky cloud-covered, no light from above. In the darkest hour of morning just before dawn, a single horn sounded. It carried through the cool moist air, over the hills, sweeping down to the fort. The sentries listened and waited.

From behind the hills, hundreds of torches rose, and came forth, igniting great bonfires on the crest of the ridge. The flames rose upward in sheets of red and orange, toward the dark sky.

As the flames grew, the dark outlines of thousands of mounted warriors became visible. They stood motionless, except for the stirring and snorting of their steeds. They held their long spears upright in a forest of lances disappearing into the blackness beyond the horizon.

Merlin had slept the day and night. And now, with the sounding of the battle horn, he was easily awakened. He heard the cries of the sentries with a mixture of fear and excitement he had never felt before. And anger. At last, an enemy in human form. The closeness of death seemed almost – a large group of men ran through the corridor past his room.

He threw on his clothes, and followed them, then climbed a ladder leading to the ramparts. As his head came through the narrow hatchway in the floor, he was blinded for a moment as his eyes adjusted from the dark hallway to the streaming rays of the dawn sun. He looked up to see Gorlois and Brennan standing completely still, their eyes fixed on the horizon. He climbed up and stood beside them.

Only a few hundred yards distant, on the ridges of the hills encircling the fort, the enemy was gathered. They formed a great half circle surrounding the eastern perimeter, twenty and thirty deep. In the center were the chiefs, on their white and black stallions – huge men seven feet tall, leaders of a hundred clans. They sat high and proud on their mounts, their horned helmets gleaming, their long moustaches trailing in thick ropes below their jaws. With leather breastplates and long fur robes covering their chests, they flaunted themselves before their enemy with savage contempt.

Surrounding them, perhaps a thousand on either side, were their clans. Their heads peered over long iron-bound wooden shields, thick arms holding long spears, muscled legs bound in leather thong; they wore long shirts of hide, their long hair blowing in the morning wind.

Next to them, on either side, the dreaded *gaesatae*, the wild men, warriors who rode into battle naked with dagger in one hand and shortsword in the other, their entire bodies painted in scenes of animals and mythical heroes. Two or three hundred held the flanks of the formation.

These were the Celtic warriors, who lived their lives devoted to the supreme moment of death in combat. Fear was unknown, contrary to all their beliefs, for they knew that a noble death sped the soul to the eternal regions, the otherworld where one might bask in the radiance of the inner sun. In the center of the chiefs, one of the leaders held a red banner draped downward on a pole cross upon which was fixed a human skull. As he began to lift it, riders pulled on reins, horses reared. A great war cry came forth from a thousand warriors, and the swarm became a torrent rushing toward the fort.

The King drew his sword. The defense had been prepared; now they could only wait.

The galloping horses stirred up a great cloud of dust that grew high into the sky. Riding, screaming, shaking their swords and spears, they came seeking valiant death.

Merlin drew his sword. The King turned toward him. "No, Merlin, I will not have a Pendragon slain within these walls."

"I must fight," Merlin protested.

"That is my command. Leave the rampart," the King ordered.

Merlin disappeared from the wall.

Suddenly the warriors reined their mounts to a stop. Out of the dust, a single man appeared, a giant over seven feet tall. His body was covered in fur robes, and he wore the head and hide of a wolf over his head. Strung over the back of his horse were two human heads embalmed in oil; they bounced as he rode. He approached within a spear's throw of the ramparts, and lifted up his voice.

"Come out now all of you," he shouted, "I will fight you alone. Winter grows near, and where am I to find more heads to soak in cedar oil, and hang from my hearth? How will I remember this season's victory? Send me a dozen men, or maybe a score. How many will you need to match my strength? My will alone could cast your fort into the sea! Come, I need heads!"

"Warrior!" It was Merlin, standing not twenty feet behind him. "Name yourself!"

Cedric whirled round.

The soldiers on the rampart looked on with astonishment, certain he was throwing his life away

The giant turned, at first startled, then moved his steed toward Merlin, and drew his sword. "I am Cedric of the Hundred Heads!"

"I am unarmed," Merlin called back, "but I call you coward

if it was your band that plundered the village three days to the south of the great mountain."

"Well spoken, little one, but you are hardly worthy of an answer," Cedric answered.

"We will see, Cedric," and in saying he turned back the inner part of his cloak to reveal the dragon brooch, mark of the Pendragon.

The giant reared back his steed. No clan would knowingly draw upon themselves the wrath of that great family.

Merlin was amused by his own gesture. It was the first time he had exercised the temporal power granted to him by his origin. His courage growing, he spoke now in a bolder tone, "So speak, are you that coward?"

The words had their intended effect; Cedric was cornered. Not even an imminent catastrophe would be forestalled by the sacrifice of personal honor. He dismounted his horse.

"I will tear you apart with my bare hands," he roared.

On the rampart nine archers drew their bows on the giant. Merlin ordered them down with a wave of his hand. Cedric was surprised by this act of courage; the boy would have little chance against him. Merlin thought quickly. He could not possibly hope for a match of strength.

He called up to the men, "A shortsword!" He caught it in his right hand while watching the movements of the giant.

Well, he might offer a little challenge after all, Cedric thought, drawing his own sword. They circled around each other, testing one another's speed with feints. Cedric rushed toward him with a great downward blow.

Merlin blocked it overhead with a clash that rung throughout his body. He drew back.

He caught Cedric's eyes, and held them. This man had killed hundreds of others, yet he could see no hatred in them. Instead there was almost a calm nobility, the valor of fearlessness.

And Cedric, too, saw something in Merlin he had never before seen, a strength drawn not from any anger, but from a tranquil inner place, like his own invincible clan leader, Alfred Strong Shoulder...

Merlin slashed toward his right side. Cedric prepared to block it, drawing his sword upright across his chest. As the swords met, Cedric felt the impact of Merlin's heel striking deeply into his belly. He gasped, doubling over into a knee slamming upward to meet his face. The blow would have knocked another man unconscious, but Cedric was only stunned, reeling slightly. But it was enough time for Merlin to throw him over backwards, laying him on the ground with a sword to his throat, his head held back by his hair.

Now with one thrust he could avenge her in a spurting of blood – but something took hold of him, held him in an iron grasp. He could not move, his eyes filled with a - whitish light. This was no killer he held, only a man living his life courageously according to his own beliefs. His anger and hatred vanished.

The evil he hoped to avenge would not be so easily found, or beaten. This was a man, nothing more; what he sought was some demon whose dwelling place he had not yet discovered.

The men still watched from above. Over the hills, the brightening of dawn cast gold light over the dark tones of the sky. A wind swept across the hill.

Merlin listened.

Had not Ioin taught him the sacredness of all life? He looked at Cedric; there was no fear in his eyes, only readiness. He discovered a voice within himself.

"I would not have your life, Cedric, for triumphs over mere mortals come easily to me, but forever beware the wrath of Cyr Myrddin!"

He drew his sword back and stood up.

Cedric looked at him with fear and amazement. Would not the watchful gods strike down any mere man that made such a boast? Now there was a burning and a

fierceness in Merlin's eyes that seemed of endless depth. Was he to believe he now lay at the feet of a god? It was not uncommon for gods to walk among men, to test their valor and courage. And if a god were to walk among men; might he not claim association with the most noble of mortal families? Who had ever before seen such power and swiftness in personal combat? He had been defeated, but not slain. And not dishonored. Indeed, was it not an honor that he had been chosen for such a battle?

Cedric returned to his warriors, bringing news of the intervention of the gods. He was believed. One third of the attackers, allies of his own clan, and many of the others, followed him back into the trackless hills, with tales of Cyr Myrddin already on their tongues. Behind them, battle horns announced the imminent siege. The remaining leaders regrouped their forces for the attack.

Merlin watched all of this with great satisfaction, then hurriedly climbed the outer wall up to the rampart. The men kept their distance; not having understood any of what had passed below, they feared some supernatural power.

But then their spirits rallied, in the realization that they were not without the favor of the gods.

The King meanwhile was concerned with more practical considerations. With the morning light he could see that many of the warriors held not spears but unlit torches in their hands. Even these noble fighters it seemed were not above evening the odds by trying to draw the battle out into open ground. There was no source of water within the stockade, and the supply would be quickly consumed in fighting a fire.

Now from behind the ranks there emerged a troop of archers, their arrows tipped by flame.

Merlin and the King entered deep into thought, knowing the threat could not be met passively. "Sire, I have an idea."

"And I have one myself," The King answered. " I have waited until their hawks were not flying." A page brought a small wooden cage to him, which he opened, withdrawing a sleek white pigeon. He kissed it, and threw it high into the air. "I prepared the message when I first heard of the coming attack."

"Sire, I need your men at my command," Merlin requested.

"You shall have them," the King replied, turning to Brennan, "Prince Merlin is acting commander."

Merlin wasted no time. "Brennan, bring all your water and wine skins into the center of the courtyard."

"At once," Brennan replied.

"And empty barrels," Merlin added.

As they brought four huge water barrels, and hundreds of skins, Merlin ordered, "Empty the water,"

Brennan looked to the King. "Sire?" The King hesitated, then nodded. The water was poured on the ground.

"Now the skins. That we may live to drink wine another day."

A crowd was gathering in the courtyard, wondering what plan Merlin had.

"Bring me oil!" he shouted. Two large barrels were rolled in. Merlin pried off their lids. "Quickly now, fill the skins." And he dipped a skin in the oil, and let it fill. A dozen pair of hands joined in. In a few moments, three hundred skins were filled.

"Rope!" A large coil was thrown down from above. Working swiftly, he tied a quick loop over each skin, and showed the men how to tie them so that the skins could be strung out along the rope in a long line, then dropped it all into the oil.

"They have lit their torches!" The sentry called out from above, as Merlin ran up the ladder to the rampart, looking to the ridge.

The warriors were riding to the bonfire by the dozen, lowering their torches into the huge flames, so that now hundreds of lights glowed brightly with the dawn.

Merlin guessed that the archers would ride first, having the greatest range. Those warriors would aim their arrows at the stockade. The torchbearers would follow, to set afire the shrub and scree that protected the ramparts from a direct assault. The wood and thatch of the houses within the stockade was too vulnerable. The archers would have to be stopped. Their usual tactic was to make a quick strike, then withdraw before the next assault force went forward, leaving time for the flames to spread, and the general havoc increase.

He would launch a counterattack.

"I need thirty archers!" The ranks filled in behind him. "And thirty swords!" These men fell in behind the others. "And thirty spears!" The spearsmen rushed forward. "And one man ready to die with me!"

The voices quieted into a murmuring, then a silence. The air grew tense. The crowd waited.

"I will go." It was Brennan."

"Good. Bring me a cart." A small hay wagon was wheeled in. "Load the skins." The skins piled high into the wagon. "Prepare formation, archers, spearsmen, then swordsmen."

"The first charge!" the sentry called down.

"Prepare to open the main gate," Merlin yelled, climbing up to the rampart. "Brennan, follow our attack as far as the main gate, then wait for me there with the cart."

A hundred archers swept across the open plain, riding furiously. Merlin watched on. He could not release his own charge until the last moment; as soon as the gates opened, the second assault force would come forth to protect the archers.

The light of morning grew golden. The approaching attack drummed a loud rumbling across the plain, and threw up a cloud of dust hundreds of feet across. He would have only two or three minutes between assaults. He could not count upon an immediate rout of the archers, but he needed the battle line far enough advanced to put his plan into effect behind the turmoil of the battle. He watched their advance, counting the seconds.

"NOW!" The gate swung open; the defenders surged forward. The attacking archers drove their mounts still faster, to reach shooting range. A dozen bows snapped. The arrows fell short of their mark, but a few reached the inner thatch roofs. But now the attack was upon them. They restrung their bows with iron tipped arrows.

The second enemy assault force charged.

Merlin jumped down from the rampart onto the wagon. He took the horse's reins and drove the wagon furiously down the hillside.

The King's archers let lose a torrent of arrows. They fell upon the enemy from above, striking fifteen or twenty, down. The archers rode to the flanks, letting the spear throwers advance.

The enemy's second charge drew near, in a brandishing of swords and spears.

The King's spearsmen hurled their missiles with deadly accuracy. Ten warriors fell pierced by the iron lances. Still the archers held their ground; throwing their bows down, they pulled out their swords. The spearsmen separated ranks; the swordsmen rushed forward for the attack.

Brennan and Merlin had reached the bottom of the hill. They pulled the skins out in a long line, spreading them more than two hundred yards across the grassy plain. The counter-attack had done its work. The swordsmen had not routed the archers, but had driven them back.

From the fort, a horn sounded. The King's troops rushed back up the hill as quickly as they had come.

The enemy archers awaited the main attack force. As the King's troops passed, Merlin called out for the wagon to be taken, and it disappeared into the stream of men, "Now hide yourself, Brennan, and good courage."

"Good faith, Merlin," Brennan responded.

Now Merlin stood alone on the plain as the charge thundered toward him. For the first time since he had formulated his plan, he looked again into the sky, observing the movements of the high clouds. The attackers were less than a minute away. He faced toward them, hoping Cedric's strange defeat might still hold some power over them. He lit the oil soaked rope that was his wick. The wick burned near to the skins. He raised his arms up slowly...Come wind, my ally, come to me in this time of need. Drive this fire into the enemy's charge. He listened. The breeze stirred, then quieted. He waited.

The first skin caught fire, burning brightly for a moment. Then it exploded in a rush of flame that waved upward in huge sheets and ran down the line, until soon a six-foot wall of fire extended a hundred yards in either direction.

On the plain, many of the warriors drew their steeds to a halt, unwilling to do battle with the gods, where honor could not be gained. But a few hundred rode on, closing the last hundred yards between themselves and Merlin. Scores of horses turned abruptly from the growing flames, pitching their riders. The others held a still fiercer rein over their mounts, denying them their very instincts. The charge rushed on. Merlin drew his sword.

The wind rose. But it was not the gentle southern breeze that had been blowing. It was a wild northern gale bearing huge black thunderheads across the horizon.

The flames whipped still higher, now advancing toward the attack. A bolt of lightning struck the plain midway

between Merlin and the charge. The horses reared. The power rose up within him, as though now his very gaze could strike the warriors down; the horses stomped nervously before his probing will. The enemy was close; he could almost look into their eyes. Time ceased to be.

One of the clan leaders dismounted, waving his sword. He marched toward Merlin in heavy strides, carrying a spear in his other hand. "We shall see whether you be man or god," he cried, and hurled his spear with a mighty heave.

Merlin deflected it so deftly it appeared to pass right through him.

"Save your spear, for earthly power too is at my command," Merlin shouted, pointing to the northern ridge. On the ridge, the King's standard flew over two thousand men – the allies had come. The warrior grunted, leaped on his horse, and led his men in flight across the hills. Merlin remained standing where he was, entranced. Brennan, on horseback, was the first to reach him.

"Merlin, are you all right?"

Merlin did not hear him. He was transfixed by the vision of his own accomplishment. This was madness; there had been no real hope of success, and yet…

"Merlin!" Brennan called, offering a hand to pull him onto the back of his horse.

He rode toward the troop that now emerged from the fort, letting Merlin dismount before riding back into battle.

Queen Ygerne rushed to him. She had watched all with apprehension, fearing greatly for Merlin's life.

"Merlin, come," she said, taking Merlin's arm. She brought him to a large chamber in the tower. "You will need your rest. Tonight there will be a great feast."

"Before the dead are buried?" Merlin asked, uneasy.

"We will observe the rights.," she answered. "I will see

you at the feast then." Ygerne left, seeking out the-King to accompany him to the feast.

Merlin remained at the window with his thoughts for a long time. Then he threaded his way through the long hallways to the feasting hall. He did not enter, but stood watching at the doorway of the torch lit chamber.

Hundreds of them with crooked elbows and huge fists grasping great clay mugs – they lifted quarts of dark beer to their thrown back heads, pouring it down their throats, banging their mugs down hard on the plank table, calling for more even as the last of their swallow dribbled down their chins and jaws. And the serving wenches, their breasts trussed high, tops uncovered, moved with trays of overflowing mugs, putting one down wherever another had just been emptied. The men grabbing at the backs of their legs as they came round, running a palm over the top of a breast, the wenches smiled and moved on; some lingered too long, were embraced and kissed and fondled, then carried off from the hall atop a broad shoulder, kicking and screaming in mock fear as the crowd laughed uproariously. One tray after another of a dozen roast ducks was dumped on the table, to disappear in a flailing of arms and heads. Above, the open flames six boars turned on the roasting spits. Loaves of black bread lay strewn across the feasting table, and on the floor. The musicians played around and around, women danced on the tables, lifting their skirts, men clapping in the rhythm as a calf was bared, a thigh, watching in unconcealed lust, until their naked legs disappeared amongst swarthy arms. Food fell from overstuffed mouths, teeth tore at roasted flesh, music swirling, clapping, stamping, cups banging, shouts and laughter…

Merlin withdrew. Air and moonlight was what he wanted. He strode out toward the northern gate.

But Ygerne had been watching him, and now followed him closely. As he approached the gate, she called, and ran to meet him. He continued walking to the gate, then turned.

"What is it, Ygerne?"

" I must speak with you."

"Then speak."

She hesitated for a moment, looking upward at the dark clouds moving across the starlit sky. Then she looked at him." Are you Cyr Myrddin, that we have heard tell of?"

The question startled him, and he turned to face her. "If I were to have the courage," he answered.

"And more than a man?" she asked.

"No, not more…"

"You always go alone. Are you not afraid?"

Merlin paused, "There is no fear beyond the gates of darkness, and through those I have already passed."

"Then what gods do you follow?" she asked.

He listened for a moment, then began slowly, "It is on these nights when somehow the shadows of starlight are more visible, and the gusts of wind know more of life...on these nights I stand in silent communion beneath the many beaconed sky, and watch the light grow on darkness's ground – but do not ask me what it is I do, for the spirit knows what it is I do, and this is my life's only reward."

"Merlin, I too have seen those gates, but I dared not approach, and now all before me seems as mere shadow." She looked into him. Take me through them," she begged.

"You must go now, Ygerne. No one has ever asked this of me – I must seek guidance. But I will come to you again." He embraced her, and vanished through the gate into the forest.

He ran in long strides, the shrubs brushing at his knees, his steps falling one after another down the hillside. At the bottom he followed a path that led into a thick glade, and

rushed into its darkness. The sounds of the night creatures were around. Small patches of moonlight shined on glowing orange mushrooms. He slowed to a walk, breathing heavily.

The forest bed was soft, covered with pine needles and rotted leaves. The air was moist and heavy, the silence ringing, waiting, exploding – an unearthly voice filled the night. His breath chilled in his throat.

And a voice, "Merlin," in a long drawn wail, "Merlin," and again the scream, not human, not animal. And again, "Merlin... "

He stopped, his breath held high in his chest like a fist. Where was his courage? Should he seek out the that voice? He did not have to decide – the voice moved toward him, wailing.

Ahead the wind blew a mist into hollow and the light of the moon filled the hovering white vapors. Forms began to appear before him, five half figures. In the center, a man's height above the ground, he saw himself, but older, weary, with long silver hair. Above his image, the face of Ygerne, below, a young boy holding a jeweled sword, on the left, a black-eyed woman with deathly smile and sharp edged necklace of gold, and on the right, a huge muscular man of great stature and long flowing yellow hair, a gaping red wound on the right side of his chest. Then it all vanished.

The Tintagel Vision of the Celtic Priesthood

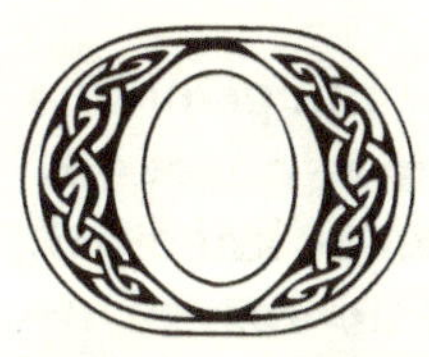

n the high cliffs of the wooded coast, the sky rises from beyond the sea's horizon climbs layered clouds to expand overhead. The wind is shining in golden red that the white gulls sail upon in their search. And they scream, the same scream that ancient seafarers heard when ending their journeys in swollen eyes and parched mouths. The trees hold the high ground; their branches stir, telling of the many wanderers who have passed below, ignorant of life in forms not human. The thin fog very distant marks the water's edge. The green of the evergreens, the blue-gray of the sky, the whitegray, the wind whipping the waves, a rushing forth in a din of cannon battering cliffs.

The sea returns ever, ancient mirror of man's beholding. The tide rises, calling all back to its waiting body, casting its voice upon the land.

Birds circle, fly upwards. Hundreds rise in an ascending spiral of wings beating, silent. They are distant, flying into where the sky is blue and silken.

To the east, the hills green and yellow and orange, colors softened in veils of mist.

To the north, now at last he could see it, a mile down the coastline. Tintagel Head. An immense spur of rock and earth, brown cliffs rising hundreds of feet from the sea, and upward to steep grassy slopes, to a small plateau. But for a narrow bridge of rock holding it to the mainland, it was an island.

Gorlois had been wise in sending him here. For it was here that the Celtic priesthood dwelled, isolated from the outer world for hundreds of years. Only in recent times had they begun to accept a few infrequent visitors. Now he would learn for himself what secret might lie hidden here. And he was in need of others on the way.

Here he might find a month's sanctuary, or even a few hours companionship. He rode the last stretch of coastline leading to the rock bridge. He dismounted and tethered his horse to a shrub. A narrow path bounded by cliffs on either side led to the gate, two huge oaken doors set with side led to the gate, two cross-pieces of iron, held in a high arched wall of stone. He knocked.

There was sound behind the gate, but no answer. He knocked again.

"Who goes there?" It was a voice that seemed unfamiliar in its role.

"It is I, Prince Merlin."

"We have no need of princes here."

"King Gorlois has sent me," Merlin said.

"Gorlois? On what errand?"

"Not one I would tell a gatekeeper."

"Then we are not obliged to allow you entrance."

"Allow me by your faith," Merlin said.

"What of your faith?" the voice asked.

Merlin hesitated. "I worship God in all men."

The gatekeeper was silent for a moment. "And where is your service given, Prince Merlin?"

"Wherever it is needed," Merlin answered.

"In war or in peace?" Yet another question.

"I have told you," Merlin insisted.

"Where have you taken your teaching?"

"From where the wind carries me, and in the valley of Llwyn Cerrig Bach."

The door was unlatched and opened by a very old man. "Your work is well known here, and well respected," the old man said.

"Then do you so love your own work that you would ask me these many questions?"

"I had to be sure it was you, and no other."

Merlin caught what seemed to be a playful glimmer in the old man's eyes. The answer had not satisfied him, but already the man had turned and begun to climb a narrow winding staircase of stone that led to the narrow winding staircase of stone that led to the plateau above.

Merlin followed.

Once on the plateau he could see ten or fifteen buildings spread over a few, acres of fields. Their walls were flat stones piled thirty or forty high. In each wall a narrow peaked arch had been cut for a window. The roofs were of stone and sod. Near the center of the cluster, he could see a well.

And beyond, in the outer field, the dark brown soil of a garden was visible.

"Where is everyone?" Merlin thought the question was simple enough.

The old man turned to him and looked into his eyes.

"Everyone?"

"The others. Are there not others?" Merlin asked.

"Oh yes, there are, others," the old man answered, speaking the last word with some amusement.

"Well?"

"I would not be too anxious about meeting them if I were you. They are not a very talkative group. In fact, they are bound by an ancient vow of silence."

"And you?" Merlin asked.

"I am not of their order," the old man answered.

"Then why are you here?" Merlin asked.

"Questions, questions. I am here of course for the same reason you are," the old man said, vexed.

Merlin withheld his next question for a moment. This old man reminded him of someone. Was it possible that..."You have known Ioin?"

The old man smiled to himself, then hesitated, as though searching his memory. "Let us discuss that another time."

"How is it that you are accepted by these priests?"

"Now that is a story as long as time itself. But I will tell you a little of it. You see, there are many different callings within one vision; we recognize another working in harmony whatever the outer appearance of his life or endeavors."

"What is this vision you speak of?" Merlin asked.

"Not yet. Come, we will eat now." He began to walk so quickly toward a large rectangular building that Merlin had to run a few paces to catch up with him. At the doorway, they ducked low to enter.

It was dim inside, and it took a moment for his eyes to adjust to the light. As his vision grew sharper, he saw thirty robed men sitting at long wooden tables and benches, eating quietly in the glow of six candles. They stopped and looked up. The old man addressed them.

"Brothers, Prince Merlin has come."

There was not a word, but the slightest nodding of heads, and in their eyes, a quiet joyful acknowledgement shining through a solemn patient wisdom.

Merlin felt a sudden stirring in his own heart, as though he now shared with each man a common depth of love and life and labor.

Two bowls of broth and black bread awaited them on the table. They sat down. His mind quieted.

His bowl was wooden, roughly carved, with a handle that had a loop of thin rope tied through it. The spoon was the same. The steam from his broth swirled and rose upward. He took his spoon in his right hand and stirred it slowly. Carrots, turnips, and melde leaves, their colors soft in the candlelight. Their aroma was rich and fragrant, like the dark soil from which they had come. He lifted a spoonful to his mouth, and sipped it, drawing a breath of air through his nose as he savored it on his tongue. The water of the broth tasted of sunlight. He chewed the vegetables slowly, and swallowed. And he felt nourished as the food became one with his body.

And all around him as well, the others were not unmindful of their partaking. Whatever their work was here, he could see it was now in their eyes. This food was taken in service to that love and labor. One by one they finished and began to leave.

He followed them outside. At a water-filled basin cut in a boulder, each man stopped to wash his bowl and spoon, before tying them to the rope around his waist.

They walked toward the western edge of the island. The sun was near setting, in layers of pastel purple and red. A slight wind blew in from the ocean, damp and salty. Near a stone and sod hut, a huge fire was burning. The men disrobed before it, entering into that hut and four others like it.

Merlin joined them in the last hut. They sat down cross-legged, on woolen mats spread over the ground. Inside it was completely dark, no windows and a low roof. Someone entered with a bucket full of red glowing rocks, and emptied them into a pit dug in the center of the hut. The air filled with their dim red light, and grew warm. A branch of sage was laid over them. It began to smoke slightly, filling the hut with its pungent aroma, while the air grew hotter beneath the low roof.

More rocks from the fire were emptied into the pit. Beads of sweat began to form on his forehead. The dry heat stung his nostrils and throat. A bowl of water was poured slowly onto the rocks, exploding into hissing and steaming. He took a deep breath; the steam pierced his lungs. The heat of the rocks burned on his shins as he tried to protect them with his hands. More water, the hut filled with steam.

In many voices, a low wail began. With their hands they slapped their legs, chests, arms in a slow rhythm. The wail became a chant, moving freely, syllables transforming, merging into one sound. The slapping grew harder, deeper, flesh unfeeling in the steam. The chanting faster. More water, steam, hissing, rocks still red and glowing in the darkness. Breathing deep, deeper, more deeply than he had ever known. One breathing, the wailing louder, finding overtones.

Water poured, steam, the air on fire, lungs burning, sweat pouring, and the chant began to slow. Their bodies became still. The rocks grew dark, then completely black.

The door flung open, and they escaped into the cool night, plunging one after another into a waist-high pool of water. Cold instantly surrounding him – a gasp! His body shook. He jumped out onto the ground, and drew a long deep breath.

His body heat returned from within, filling his chest and limbs with a warm fiery glow. The earth at his feet was still cold. Overhead, the sky had turned black, filled with thousands of brilliant points of light. The steam rose from his skin. The ocean waves crashed far below. The wind gusted. The limbs of an evergreen danced, twisting and swirling, heaven above, earth below, alive, alive. Light in his eyes, the wind on his body, the soil at his feet, this breath his very first, this moment its own revelation. Heaven above, earth below, and his body the very altar of their communion. And the flesh, was good, and it was strong.

They began donning their robes, moving forth to form a circle around the fire. The wind shook the branches while the silence grew louder, the stars brighter, and the earth stronger. The light descended. It passed amongst them, whirling around and around the circle, filling the ground itself with its life. His head grew faint; he almost fell. Then it was over.

The men returned to their sleeping huts. Merlin was shown a pile of straw. He lay down, and slept.

In a small boat with her, he approached the dark shore. The boat grounded on the rocks. They began wading in the waves.

Twilight comes the archer. She is all powerful. With one swift arrow both their hearts are pierced, and they fall beside each other on the shoreline, with the waves washing over their bodies.

But still they breathe; their wounds are gone. At last they have reached the land. Lying on their backs, moonlight on their upturned faces. The archer is not evil. And the wind at twilight sails ever on.

The priest of the last night-watch awoke them before dawn.

In the moonlight, Merlin could see a thin trail of mist moving through the open window. The sound of the surf was strong, but distant. The smell of the air was saltier than before. They pulled their long wool robes over themselves, and walked the trail that led to the center of their small settlement, to the well.

Each took a cup of water, drank it slowly, then walked over to the grass and sat facing east.

For a long time they were silent.

At last the night began to depart; the stars grew dim. The sky turned silver, red, orange. The gulls flew low overhead. The sun began to rise over the hilly plain, a clear yellow orb. When its complete circle was visible, they entered into the chapel, a hut of flat piled stones.

The eldest took his place behind the altar. The others kneeled on stone benches. On the altar were two lit candles, and a book. The priest opened it, and began to read. Dust stirred slowly in the sun's rays coming through the windows.

"Sa tus bhi an Briathar ann, ague bhi an Briathar in einecht le Dia, ague ba a Dia an Briathar. Is e a bhi ann i dtus ama in eineacht le Dia; is trisdean a cruthaiodh gach ni agus ina eagmais-sean nior cruthaiodh aon ni da ndearnadh. Is ann a bhi an bheatha, agus ba i an bheatha

solas an chine dhaonna. Bion an solas ag soilsiu sa dorchadas, ages nil bua ag an dorchadas air."

"In the Beginning was the Word, and the Word was with God, and the Word was God. The same was in the Beginning with God. All things were made by Him; and without Him was not anything made that was made. In Him was life, and the life was the light of men. And the light shineth in darkness, and the darkness comprehended it not."

He continued the sermon in the ancient tongue. When the service was complete, each man went to take up his labor for the day. Merlin was left alone, standing before the chapel door. He decided to wander around the perimeter of the plateau. He walked until he came to a grassy slope. He lay down on the grass to watch the clouds' creations overhead.

Surely there must be more, he thought. But perhaps those secrets are not as easily given out. For now, I have nowhere else to go, so I will remain, and listen.

The hours passed. He explored more of the settlement. In the afternoon he sat in meditation, watching the sun begin its slow descent toward the horizon. At sunset, he returned again to the eating place, to find the gatekeeper awaiting him at the doorway.

"Prince Merlin," he said, "if you will let your hunger pass, we will speak more."

"Very well," Merlin answered.

"Come, then," he said.

Merlin followed him to a small hut. They entered it and sat down on the wooden floor near one corner. The old man lit a candle and held it up between them so that he could see Merlin's face.

"You do not know who I am, do you?" the old man asked, causing Merlin to shake his head.

"I am Melchar," he continued, stopping to see if this drew forth a response from Merlin, but Merlin said

nothing. "Oh well, I thought Ioin might have told you," Melchar smiled.

"Then you do know Ioin," Merlin asked.

"Oh yes, Ioin was my teacher as well," Melchar said.

"Does he still live in the hills, Melchar?"

"Now that is a question not easily answered. But it was indeed a great fortune that he allowed you to come to him, made possible by his grace alone, and his knowledge of the realms."

"I do not understand," Merlin questioned.

"I would not venture to explain it further. But it is a great omen."

"He is still alive?" Merlin asked.

"He is not where any of us could easily find him."

"I could find him," Merlin offered.

"You know not what you say," Melchar warned.

"Is he dead then?" Merlin was becoming upset. "You forget his teaching."

"What teaching do you –"

"Some last words perhaps... 'The boundaries of the living and the dead are not as commonly seen..." Melchar smiled softly, opening his eyes wide.

"What!?" Merlin exclaimed, shocked by the recounting of Ioin's words, searching in Melchar's eyes for an answer.

Melchar put his hand over Merlin's heart. "Some day, young brother, all this will be given over to your understanding. But there is more. Do I have your trust? ""

Merlin nodded, still very much bewildered.

"Merlin, you were raised a Christian?"

Merlin nodded.

"And hold to the teachings of that faith?" Melchar asked.

"I abide by his teaching, and not by what words other men would make his," Merlin answered.

"You speak of the Christ?"

"Call him what you will," Merlin said.

"He was the Son of God," Melchar spoke.

"And so we are all. By his own words, he said, 'You are Gods'," Merlin replied

"What of his words, 'I am the Way, the Light, and the Truth'?"

"He spoke true. God is the voice and vision of our own true Self," Merlin said.

"Few would understand it so," Melchar replied.

"I fear you are right, Melchar."

"We are not all strong; we hold to the image of one man who was not unfaithful to the spirit within him," Melchar advised.

"And so are unfaithful to our own spirit," Merlin said.

"Not always. The ways of the power are unfathomable. In time it brings all within its realm, but in many different ways," Melchar countered.

"Why worship the man, and not the spirit?" Merlin questioned.

"How many can worship what does not have human form? The spirit's realm is often frightening to traverse, and one takes comfort in the guidance of a human voice," Melchar answered.

"I find my kinship in the kingdom of the starlit night," Merlin said.

"Do not be so harsh, Merlin. This is a land of leaders. The people need a figure of loyalty and devotion, one who upholds the new faith."

"A man who lived four centuries ago cannot unite the clans, or halt the barbarian invasion," Merlin spoke.

"Perhaps not, but his spirit embodied in a warrior of near equal greatness, a warrior king –"

"You speak not of Uther or Ambrosius, for I fear they are but Romans in their hearts," Merlin objected.

"I speak not of them." Melchar stopped for a moment. The silence grew heavy. "Do you not know where you

go? I speak not of them, but of one who will come after them."

"Then who?" Merlin demanded.

"He is yet to be born," Melchar answered.

"It is a distant hope then," said Merlin, shaking his head. " The Saxon threat is upon the tribes. Their way of life is already near crumbling."

"No, it is far more than a hope." Melchar grew solemn. "For this sanctuary has stood for four centuries, and for four centuries the vision has grown. Now the time of waiting grows short, and the time of fulfillment is at hand."

"Then your prayers have been for this warrior?"

"More than prayers. More than a warrior. More. Meditations, studies, chants. For four hundred years Tintagel has been inhabited with but one purpose, and every hour of every day has been dedicated to the forging of this one vision, unbeknownst to the generations of kings that have passed."

Merlin was silent for a moment. "And you tell me all this, Melchar?"

"There is one thing that is certain, Merlin, you have been within the circle before, and you will yet be with us when you leave," Melchar said.

"You think me part of this work?" Merlin asked.

Melchar drew a breath and nodded. "Let me tell you of a passage from our sacred books. Sometime after the massacre at Anglesey, near the turn of the first century, a high Druid made a prophesy. It was this: When the great city falls, and the island weakens, the falcon will come from the north. And the lords of war will join with him to create the unseen foundation of a nation that will become the strongest in all the world, and nowhere will its flag be unknown."

"It is a great prophesy," Merlin said.

"And the answer to your question," Melchar replied.

"What question?" Merlin asked.

"Hear me. Llwyn Cerrig Bach, to the north. Merlin, the smallest of our native falcons," Melchar said.

Merlin stopped, collecting his thoughts. "Can it be so," he whispered, his breath suddenly holding high in his chest.

"It is so, Merlin," Melchar continued, "you are yet young, but soon it may seem the weight of the world is upon you. Try to remember that you are not alone."

"Not alone?" Merlin pondered.

"He who having once put his hand to the plow, looks back, is not worthy of the harvest. Courage, young Merlin" For a long time neither of them spoke.

Finally Merlin addressed Melchar as if in a trance. "And the warrior king?"

"The falcon roams far and high over the land, seeing all. Use the power that has been granted you, Merlin. The seed of a nation is in your hand."

"And the name of the one who comes?"

"Arthur, the bear," Melchar answered.

"Arturus. I too will pray for the coming of the bear," Merlin said.

"Only remember, Merlin, our dreams are not endless, nor all powerful. That is why in this life there can be only one dream, and the heart, the mind, and the will must all be consumed in this one fire."

"I know it too well," Merlin spoke.

"Go with Him, then," Melchar said.

"And with you always," Merlin replied.

Merlin left through the narrow door, crouching so as not to strike his head. His heart and mind now filled with a great new excitement, and a great new fear. Had destiny so marked him? Would he be worthy of his calling?

He wandered out into the open fields beneath the stars. And the spirit filled him. I am free, born of this moment

and no other. And father to more ahead. I hold the stars in my hand, no longer lost. I am born again from the ashes of my own body. Communion! The night sings. It roars. The stillness is on my tongue. I swallow the silence. Rain, heaven's precious gift. Live the beginning. Live the end. We are held in the embrace, the one embrace of all holding, for it is over uncharted seas that the wind blows strongest!

And to turn away from a doorway leaves one with nothing.

Wind, you are my guardian, and my confessor. Darkness, you are my most faithful companion.

And I know, beyond the touched, beyond the world, there is a place, there is a place. Night spirit invade! Night spirit invade! Night spirit invade!

His hands opened, fingers spread, shot upward on up stretched arms. Fire! He stood like a spire of rock. The light rose up within him, in a fire that devoured the gates of past and future. And all life and creation was before him, and all was his.

He stood on the highest part of the sloping fields, the clouds in great moonlit towers above him, as the wind began to stir, to sweep, to rage and explode. Fire! The gateway to the kingdom.

And he knew he must leave this very moment. He strode into the empty hut where he had left his belongings, then rushed out to the gate.

It was deserted, but leaning across the oak doors was a freshly carved staff. Its head was the head of a dragon, its foot a dragon's foot. Melchar's gift. He took it and let himself out through the gate 'Farewell, Melchar, I will return again to Tintagel.'

He walked the trail into the mountains, climbing upon the high ridges. Far below was another valley, churning in mist, some light from fires, a few houses visible, a stone bridge over a stream. The mist was

rising within itself. A jagged spear of lightning silently illuminated a distant mountain. High in the air, a hawk flew on an updraft, gliding higher and higher in an ascending spiral.

His spirit was uplifted; his pace was smooth and strong. He walked through the night, through the dawn, and by midday he knew his destination.

An uneven conical hill appeared seemingly from nowhere to rise more than six hundred feet above the flat plain. It was called Camulodunum. Its lower portions were shrouded in trails of mist, but its summit was clearly visible, a high grass-covered mound a few hundred yards square.

He did not know what power it was that drew him there, but he walked the entire afternoon, and late into the evening to reach it. Now it was nearing midnight. The sky was clear and black, but the stars were hidden from him by the low fog. He began the climb. The way was not difficult, but he was weary, and as he rose higher he was exposed to the cold blasts of wind.

He walked upward, the summit receding before him.

At last he reached the top.

He walked slowly around the few hundred yards of its perimeter. Below, the smaller hills on the horizon pushed upward like islands through the sea of fog that spread for miles in all directions. Above, the stars were shining clear. He grew silent within, and sought guidance. It was his own voice that came forth.

'As in any room there is a place of power where one must stand, so on any countryside there is a hill that rises above the rest, and in any nation, there is a countryside that holds the keys to the kingdom. This then will be my first gift to you, Arturus, young bear – an island of power where you may find right dominion over the empire, and sacred communion with the stars.

Above all mortal pathways, mounted only in deep worship, here will be an island inviolate of the veiling mists. By night, it will ride above, a lake of moonlight in the clouds, where the shadows of all things to be will find haven, and be given succor. Here, my unborn king, you will find your beginning, your kingdom, and perhaps, your end.'

Windgate,
Hill Passage

ranches stir, shaking, clattering. Wind rushes, churns, caresses, weeps and howls. Exploding, it lays down, laughs, dances, climbs, begins, touches, plays, lives, threatens, dies, is reborn, comes to him, makes peace, finds silence, understands, awakens.

He had no knowledge of where he was going, or being taken. But he knew when it was time to move on, to make one more step toward the unknown destination ahead. What he left behind became only a many faceted crystal within his mind, a still and frozen panorama that awaited the addition of each new experience, but that was somehow gone forever.

He came to live with the horizon; each day was a sacrifice to the sun ever setting in the low lying hills. It was all that was important, this calling that brought strength to his heart, and allowed him no rest. But now each day was sanctified, because he had found his life in the fortress beyond ignorance. He moved within his own gentleness, in the eye of the storm; high winds surrounded him, and still he felt young.

But there was much he did not understand. At night it would begin, the dreams that came before sleep, feelings of sharing presence with those who were not there, a sense of traveling freely through the past and the future, knowing where he had been centuries ago, where he would be in as many years ahead. The land he walked became a foreign land, where the laws of the ordinary world were not encountered, and so could not limit.

Still, his heart grew weary from moving place to place. He would return home, if he knew where that would be. He would go to be embraced by a woman waiting, if he knew where that would be. He would lie down in his own bed in peace and comfort if somewhere there was a home that could not be taken from him.

But he had nowhere to lay his head, except on the earth; she alone would not desert him in his wanderings. Day and night lost all importance to the rhythm of his life; the world turned wholly within him. He listened for hours at a time, searching for the next movement of the wind, awakening often in the middle of the night to set out for an unknown place, losing the path, regaining it, waiting until sunrise to determine a course over a mountain or through a river valley.

But deeply within himself, he knew he would continue northward. A journey seeks its roots; he would find Ioin, and tell him all that had happened.

Autumn still lit the hillsides. Pastures and forests of emerald green turned brown and gold and red. The air was thick and musty with the smells of rotting vegetation. The ground was soft with a blanket of damp leaves, and the night air golden, clear, crisp, and sweet. The scent of berries carried on the moist wind.

The great flocks flew southward.

On the moorlands, the grasses flamed gold and rust and purple. Toadstools sprouted from the forest bed, and frost came in the night.

Now at last, after the long months of journeying, he could once again see the familiar mountains. Their peaks were veiled in a glow of golden fog, and above them, orange gold fleecy clouds, a few gray white, tinted purple. The low hills before them were almost black, their edges gilded by the setting sun, and the fog all around was alive with the light coming over the mountains.

He approached the village that lay several miles from the foothills. Already word had reached the villagers that Prince Merlin of the Pendragon, whom many now called Cyr Myrddin, was traveling north.

By the time he had reached the outskirts, hundreds had gathered along the road. He put his black stallion into a trot, and rode down the main lane with his gaze fixed straight ahead.

The villagers watched on quietly, sensing he would brook no interference. He rode on toward the outer hills.

His mind began to fill with apprehension and excitement. Would Ioin be there still? It had not been so long...but had he been faithful to his teaching? Ioin could see into his innermost fears and struggles. He could only wait to find out.

He took the miles slowly, watching all that passed. But as he drew closer, the countryside became less familiar. The trail took him through groves and pastures he did not remember.

He approached the tiny hamlet that lay just a few miles below the cave. He went first to find their garden, where he had shared so many mornings with Ioin.

It was nowhere to be found. A stand of tall yew trees covered the ground where he remembered it to be. Had he so forgotten the terrain he had walked only a year ago? On a nearby field, he saw a farmer tending his crop, and ran over to him.

"I am looking for a garden. It was over there, in those trees."

"There are no gardens around here," the farmer answered.

"It was on that very spot. I used to tend it."

The man gave him a queer look. "You must be mistaken."

Merlin drew back, confused.

"Wait. I do remember something. My grandfather used to tell me about his younger days. Told me once there was an old hermit living back in those hills. He had a garden down here. Most kept their distance from him, but the children liked him, and they called him Old Silver, because of his long gray hair and beard. He played with them, acted just like a child himself, they say."

"What became of the old man?"

"I guess he just stopped coming down one day. Right in the middle of the harvest they say. Funny thing though."

"What is that?"

"Seems the story about the old man was around even before my grandfather. Guess it's a legend."

Merlin was not able to make much sense of the farmer's words, but he asked one more question. "Did the old man ever come here with another?"

"For a time, there was a young man who helped him in the garden. But he was killed by a Roman soldier who took him for an outlaw. They say the old man took it hard, was never the same again. Not long after that he stopped coming down into the valley."

Merlin handed the man a few coins.

"Tend my horse until I return," Merlin said.

He began to walk into the hills to find the cave. The landscape was still unfamiliar. The trail brought him through completely different groves and hollows, but at last he could see the dark opening of the cave on the hillside. He ran up close to its mouth, listened for a moment, and then shouted, "Ioin!"

Inside, something stirred. He walked a few steps closer. A low growl came forth from the darkness. Quietly he threw off his cloak, winding it around his right forearm. He began to step back. It came into the light, snarling. He braced himself – the wolf attacked. He fell back beneath its weight, keeping his forearm at his throat, the fury over him, tearing at his arm, trying to reach the vulnerable flesh of his neck. Before it could find his throat, he placed his other arm behind its neck, and forced his forearm into its upper jaw. As the wolf bit at him savagely, he withdrew into himself, dismissing the pain and all fear, and called up all his strength. He pushed back harder and harder, straining every muscle,

bending its head back against the neck until it cracked. The wolf spasmed and fell limp on top of him. He let his arms and head drop to the ground, and rested, panting. He pushed the body off of him He rolled over onto his hands and knees, trying to catch his breath, then stood, stumbling to a nearby shrub. He broke off some of its branches to fashion a torch, and entered the cave. It was empty, no signs of recent habitation. But sounds came from the back chamber, whimpering. He approached. The torch cast its light on two small wolf cubs, snuggling against one another. He picked them up in his arms, and held them against his chest.

"Now pups, we have only each other," he said.

He listened as the night wind passed before the cave entrance, howling.

He laid the cubs down again on his cloak, and covered them. The air began to grow cold and damp. The wind quieted. He took his blanket, pulled it over himself, and slept. Outside, snowflakes began to fall.

In the morning when he awoke, he knew this would be where he would winter. He would have to obtain grains from the villagers, and gather his store of wood for the long cold months ahead. Then he remembered. The hidden chamber!

He went to it and pulled aside the large stone slab that covered the entrance. He took a torch and entered. The chest was not there. The chamber was empty. He turned to go out, but then caught a glimpse of something lying in the dust. He picked it up, a small bible.

The day passed quickly, and at nightfall exhaustion came to him. As he sat by the flames of his fire, he thought of the time he would spend here. He had wanted to be alone; he could not ask for a deeper solitude than what now lay before him. And although the days now grew cold and wet, the cave offered him its own kind of warmth, and haven from the snow-covered land.

The weeks passed. The wolf cubs grew less fearful and began to play, at first with each other, and then with him. They carried sticks to him, holding them fast in small teeth, growling and challenging him to try to take them away. When they wanted affection, they would roll on their backs, offering him their soft bellies to rub. He was grateful for the companionship, taking the opportunity to learn everything he could about their ways.

Occasionally a villager ventured up to the cave with some small gift of grain or milk, or a bit of mutton, but he ate hardly at all, fasting for days at a time. Much of the food he would give to the cubs.

Usually, the villagers left their offerings at the mouth of the cave, not wanting to disturb him, but today, near twilight, Merlin was sitting outside when a man came to bring him a pouch of milk.

He approached slowly, as though unsure of himself. As he drew closer, Merlin could see that his face was in some way disfigured.

"Do not be afraid, friend. Come here." He needed a better look at the man; the air had grown dark. Merlin went into his cave, motioning for the man to follow him. He shook his head, but then approached a few steps closer to the cave's entrance. Merlin returned with a torch. He held the light up to the man's face. His lips were swollen and bleeding, his face covered with dull bluish spots.

"As I thought. Do others in the village have this same sickness?" Merlin asked.

"Every winter it comes to many on the cold winds."

Merlin smiled. "Here, take this." He handed him a large pouch, as the man looked at him questioningly.

"Dried violets. Chew several every day and you will be healed. And share them with the others."

The man thanked him, bowed his head, and withdrew.

Not long after, the gifts to Merlin began to increase, and more sought him out to be healed. He treated them all,

some with his own gathered medicines, some with the fresh herbs and roots he was able to find in the area. He taught them how to find and prepare their own medicines, and so became well loved amongst them.

But his loneliness would not easily leave him. Still he was alone in his work. For now, all was quiet, and no guidance was forthcoming. These mornings he would awaken with the sunrise, walk down to the lake with a vase, and bring back his day's supply of water. Along the way he would gather greens for his meals, and pick up a few pieces of wet wood to dry by his fire. He cooked his grains all day in an iron kettle that had been given to him by an old woman from the village. But mostly he waited, and listened to the rain. The effort of keeping himself warm seemed to fill the day. It was enough.

So he continued on into the dead of winter. Night after night he sat beside his fire, waiting but not knowing why, watching the wolf cubs grow strong, until the time came when the days stopped growing shorter. With this first sign of the approaching spring, thoughts and feelings began to stir deep inside him.

This evening, he stood watching the amber sun sinking below the hills, leaving the air with a golden gray aura, and tinting the white shadows of snow on the trees. He breathed the quiet, and then returned into his cave, and to his fire.

As he looked into its flames, images came to him, one after another, that he had not called forth. The face of Branwen appeared, of his mother, of Ygerne. They swirled together, circling; one after another grew large in the foreground. The images possessed him.

What has all this love been that has come to me? Was it only a fleeting dream, hoping to have her by my side?

Or any woman*? ...now he was over her, the length of his body against her nakedness. His toes brushing against the bottoms of her feet, his knees sliding beside her thighs, bellies pressed together, moving his chest over the tips of her breasts, his arms lying on her arms outstretched beyond her head, fingers holding fingers.*

His lips parted hers, silken wetness; his eyes held hers in asking.

He moved his hands down her arms, over the delicate roundness of her shoulders, beneath their hollows to lift with his fingers the sides of her breasts, to caress their brown tips, to cup their flesh in his palms as he brought the warmth of his mouth to cover one and then another, his lips opening, sliding over them. Her body arched up, ward, pressing her pelvis into his. He traced the sides of her ribs with his hands, lower and lower, up over the curving hips, gently down the smoothness of her lower belly, over the dark moist hair, his hands between her legs, through the heat of her inner thighs, then running to hold her legs behind her knees, lifting them outward parting her thighs, pushing them back until his arms could bend around them, and his fingers return over her hips and down her belly to part that red opening into her, to enter her with himself.

Her legs wrapped around him, holding as he thrust into that darkness, the rhythm of their bodies in increasing circles as she took him from his search, to give him warmth and peace and child, the sweet bitterness of knowing in this one moment was his own immortality sacrificed to woman, to the flesh around his flesh, and the ground beneath them...

He awoke into his turmoil, with the dream still lying close. Now all his work ahead seemed only a shadow, hollow and without fulfillment, if this, his one gift to life in return for the life granted him, was not to be received. The blood of his heart and throat and eyes ran full in his belly and loins. All seemed a cruel jest, and the sacrifice too great. He had given himself over to life that life would be fulfilled, and made more abundant. But now it seemed he would not be called as all men were called. To dance and drums, forest and drums, woman, woman, woman.

He would lie with the earth alone, and she would take his life, as he wanted it to be taken. And would this child not be born of flesh and blood, but of mere ethereal dream? An unknown creature, formless, inhuman? He was being raped, by the night, by no woman. Her womb claimed his loyalty; she was without mercy and allowed him no other. He wept in the love that had brought him to this place, that had taken his life, that he had willingly given.

There was no returning. Could he watch his calling vanish like the morning mist, to find his light in the eyes of his children, and a woman? He had chosen in full knowledge, seeing all that would be left behind, but the choice was not made once and completed. It became a choosing, the intensity of the struggle ever searching him out. Again and again the love of his heart would appear before him, and he would reach out to touch her, but in the moment of touching knew he could not continue. It was a dream that could never be more. Of his vision, now all was lost but the choosing that allowed him no way but his destined way, his chosen unfoldment, chosen before he was born, chosen by him, chosen by his ancestors, chosen by life. Joy was sorrow was suffering, to touch was to sever, to behold was to become blind, to love was to leave...

Where he had touched her breasts and thighs now cold stones lay underneath him, and before him, the embers and low flames of the fire. The flames burned in his small circle of stones, danced upward. He could not sleep, only lie empty. The warmth of the fire was diminishing, its light only a soft flickering in a place that seemed all darkness. Not even his mind could imagine him not alone. Apart, apart from himself, apart from others, apart from everything.

His aloneness was a stone in his belly. The flames died. A few more hours of unwilling sleep brought him to the crest of dawn.

Clouds were massing on the horizon, billowing and dark, growing up-ward thousands of feet in rolling towers. The wind reached into the cave, a soft hollow whistle bringing the damp and musty air. Leaves stirred on branches. Light that was not the sun flickered in the clouds; dawn shadows disappeared for an instant, then returned again in gray and brown. The wind swirled faster, laden with moisture. A few huge drops, one after another, hit the dirt in front of the cave, but when at last the tribes of thousands issued forth from the sky, he was again asleep, and the wetness could not chill him.

He awoke with a cool wetness on his downward cheek, saliva from the corner of his mouth. His body was hot despite the cold drafts passing under his blankets.

Somewhere distant, a wild dog howled, or wailed. The night had been long, its journeys difficult. Much was changing; much was being left behind; much was dying.

Yet something was being born as well.

Outside the cave it was raining hard, in a steady pouring on the rock face. The air was turbulent, stirring, rolling. High above, thunder trembled in a low voice, grew closer, finally exploding all around.

Through the narrow opening in the rock he saw a single fork of lightning crack the sky with its white fire.

The air filled with dampness around him, but he had blankets, and a roof of rock to shelter him from the raging sky.

He reached into his carrying bag and withdrew the small worn bible. He opened it. In barely legible script

he read, *"Yr hwn sydd yn trigo yn nirgelwch y Goruchaf, a erys y'nghsgod yr Hollaluog.*" "He who dwells in the Secret Place of the Most High shall abide forever in the Shadow of the Almighty." He took comfort, and read for the rest of the day.

When night came, he slept.

In the morning he was awakened by a voice calling to him from down below on the trail.

"Prince Merlin, are you there?"

He went to the cave's entrance. "Who calls?"

"The royal messenger of the Pendragon."

"Come up then," Merlin called back.

The messenger hurried up the hillside.

"What is it, messenger?" Merlin asked.

"King Uther calls you to thc royal court in Old Amesbury."

"Amesbury? For what reason?" Merlin asked.

"None is given, your grace." The messenger looked around, somewhat confused to find a Pendragon living in a cave.

"Is there anything else?" Merlin wanted to know before dismissing him.

"Yes, this ring." He handed it to Merlin. "With it you will find protection, and all that you will need for your journey."

"Protection?" Merlin laughed to himself. "Very well, when the snow runs then."

"When the snow runs." The messenger left.

Merlin spent the next weeks preparing for his journey. His wolf cubs had left him, eager to explore new territories. He packed away his stores of food in the rear chamber along with some of the articles he had accumulated during his stay.

It came time for him to depart. He threw on a long black cloak.

He would return first to the sea, and seek guidance, before going to meet Uther. He traveled for three days to the coast.

The sea was alive, alive in white-crested hills that cast great trailing sheets of mist downwind, and broke in long curving lines over the beach, exploding upward, layer upon layer like a thousand white-maned horses surging toward the shore.

A gull beat its wings furiously to fly a few feet forward into the wind, was thrown back, struggling ahead; it held motionless in the air, wings beating.

A few massive clouds were outlined against the solid gray sky. The wind beat his cloak as he leaned forward to hold his balance, stiffening against the gusts that were let loose between mere seconds of steady wind. Tiny stones stung his face; sand and small sticks flew by.

He walked down the beach, the salty mist in his eyes and face. The water poured and crashed, the wind thundered, and the taste of salt was on his lips. The gray, green horizon fell away into the mist. He took out his pouch and withdrew from it the ring of the Pendragon.

He examined it in the twilight. So I am born of this noble family, this mortal family, under the mark of the dragon. But why? It seems that life does not suit me. Yet...so it is...

Come forth dragon, hide no longer as the banner of kings!

Dragon! Symbol of the darkness that reveals, dweller at the threshold, guardian of gateways, of kingdoms impassable except to the strongest, whom death cannot possess, in whom fear can find no dwelling. Dragon! Slayer of the unworthy, lover of the dying, lord of the wards, peacemaker, fire king, demon of laughter, of eternal smoke. Fire! Fire! Fire! Fire! Denizen!

Windgate, Hill Passage

Now the wild dance of wind was all around. In the sky, the clouds' fury rising in black mountains, deep valleys, molten silver pouring over hills in the heavens, shaded gray furrows – the low naked moon flew to and fro. A low growl rattled in his throat, like a trapped animal, his steps impulsive, striding forward, listening, trying to grab hold, slamming his feet on the ground, pacing back and forth, lunging in one direction and then another, three steps here, two steps there, four step here, forward. Back. Aside.

At last the stars came, breaking through night in soft explosions, banishing the clouds with breaths of light.

So I am a Pendragon. And it is well, for the destiny of the family is well watched.

It was that winter that Hengist, leader of the Saxons, offered peace and perpetual friendship to King Vortigern, ruler of the eastern territories. King Vortigern took council, and decided to accept the proposal. It was agreed that a delegation from each side would meet without arms to seal the new treaty.

A huge feast was prepared. The foremost men of the clans sat down in friendship, each Saxon with a Briton beside him.

When all were seated, Hengist shouted an arranged signal. "Saxons, take your axes!"

Each Saxon drew his knife and attacked his neighbor. The Britons struggled courageously, but without weapons they were soon overcome. Over three hundred of the counselors and officers of Vortigern were murdered. Vortigern himself was captured, and released only after he had promised the Saxons more territory.

Early that spring, King Uther and his brother Ambrosius discussed Vortigern's plight.

"How fares Vortigern?" Uther asked.

"This summer must surely be his last. The treachery of the long knives has left him without officers," Ambrosius answered.

"Then his army will be vanquished, and Hengist will sweep the south," Uther pronounced.

"Already peasants and soldiers flock to my kingdom, knowing Vortigern must fall," Ambrosius added. "We are the last fort of the civilized way. And our families and homes, too, will soon lie under the threat of the barbarians. Slavery or death awaits us all if we do not stand strong."

"And this Roman island will be no more. The roads and buildings of the conquered lands have already fallen into disrepair, temples destroyed," Uther said.

"It will be our greatest and most perilous hour. The Roman way must prevail. Our men will fight with valor behind the standards of our legions, our allies – "

"You will need more," a voice said. Uther and Ambrosius turned to see Merlin entering the chamber.

Ambrosius spoke for himself and his brother. "Welcome, Prince Merlin, we trust your journey has been a safe one."

"It could not have been otherwise," Merlin said.

"Yes...you must know why we have called you here. The civilized kingdom lies under threat of invasion. All forces are being gathered under the banner of the golden dragon. You are a Pendragon, as we, fed your first food on the tip of a sword."

"Ambrosius, we know our own heritage well. Surely you have not brought me these many miles for idle talk."

Ambrosius, surprised by Merlin's tone, looked to Uther, who only smiled. Ambrosius continued. "Prince Merlin, it is said, you…"

"Have some special gifts." Uther finished the sentence for his brother. "We desire your counsel on our cause."

Merlin nodded, meeting each of their eyes in turn, contemplating his answer.

"In the joining of arms there is more, more than stratagems and the instruments of war. It is not men, but human spirit itself that wars on the battlefield. Ambrosius, consider this: Your army is the old army of Britain. Your men obey your officers because of discipline. The warriors of your enemy are bound to their officers in kinship and loyalty. Your troop weakens when its leader falls; theirs is strengthened tenfold. For if one of their clan leaders falls, his men cannot return home except in disgrace; they stand and fight until their death."

"Go on, I am listening," Ambrosius said.

You fight for a way of life; they fight for adventure. You bring your men to war with promises of glory; Hengist leads his men with promises of riches and booty. It is shameful for them to earn by sweat what they can win by blood – "

"But our men hearken to trumpet and bugle," Ambrosius interrupted. "They fight in mobs; we form in ordered lines of cohorts. And my men rally to the en-signs of their legions."

"Symbols of a dying order. It is not enough. In the meeting of arms, violent emotion fights stronger than vague ideal."

"Have we any other path to follow?" Uther asked.

"There is something greater than either of these. Even now I sense its approach." Merlin's thoughts turned suddenly inward. "I speak of something that would unite all the tribes of the island."

"What? That has never been done," Uther said, and then added, "Never *will* be done."

Merlin stopped, changing his tone. "My journey leaves me weary. By your leave?"

"Your chamber has been prepared," Ambrosius

answered, watching Merlin as her turned to leave, taking measure of the man.

"Merlin?" Uther's call stopped him at the doorway. "I should like to see you again in the evening."

"I am at your service, King Uther," Merlin responded, bowing slightly before closing the door behind himself.

Ambrosius turned to his brother. "The young prince is wise, but speaks some in riddles. What is the meaning of this last part?"

"I think he speaks of the gods."

Ambrosius laughed, but more in despair. "Prayers and rosaries against a sword?"

"I would not dismiss his knowledge so lightly," Uther said.

"I will consider what he has said of the troops, but disregard the rest," Ambrosius said.

"Brother, do not be so hasty. There are forces that move men…" Uther advised.

"If it is of importance to you, make it your concern. My men need only their flag. I go to council."

Uther nodded and Ambrosius left.

That evening Uther went to Merlin's chamber. He found Merlin sitting on a deerskin before a roaring fire. Merlin spoke to him as he entered, without turning his gaze from the flames. "What you have come to ask of me should not be asked of any man, but I will hear you."

Uther strode into the room, unsure of a response. He decided to answer in a straightforward manner. "It is not as you would imagine."

"Speak then," Merlin said.

Uther sat down beside him. He looked at the profile of Merlin's face. The flames flickered in shadows and colored light across his skin. Then he too turned his gaze into the hearth. "All my life, Merlin, I have been a warrior, a man of action. Now I have come to something that is beyond understanding. I have never known much

of love, but now I am as one possessed. It is not mortal beauty alone that draws me to Ygerne. There is something-"

"Ygerne!?" Merlin exclaimed.

"You know her then?" Uther responded, equally surprised.

Merlin recovered from his momentary shock. "I may," he answered, collecting his thoughts.

"When I am with her I feel more like a wind in the heavens than a man. You may call it passion, but in all my years, if I have ever known anything, it is that I must have her. I must lie with her. I must lie with her, Merlin."

Merlin just looked at him, keeping his counsel.

"Merlin, I...have often made light of the magical arts, but now I sense you alone can help me. You know of these things, your journeys..."

Merlin turned toward Uther. His face was worn and battle-hardened, and yet graced by a simple wisdom. He had come in good faith.

"And Ygerne, does she return your favor?"

"I am sure of it," Uther said without hesitation. "I must put myself in your hands."

"For how long have you felt this love?"

"Only days, since I have seen her at the eastern council."

"You would have me betray Gorlois?"

"Can real love ever be a betrayal?" Uther asked.

"I will need time, to consider," Merlin said.

Uther drew back into his noble military bearing, unable to remain any longer at ease. "I will be back in an hour."

"You will be back in the morning," Merlin directed.

Their eyes met, the eyes of two very different kinds of warriors.

"In the morning then." Uther left.

Windgate, Hill Passage

Merlin found himself alone again with the fire. Already he knew. He would help Uther.

In the morning Uther came to him, and awaited his word.

"This is not an easy thing for me, Uther, but I will help you – if you can promise me one thing."

"Ask, and I will grant it," Uther said.

"That if a child is born of this union, it will be given over to my care."

Uther looked at him. "Granted."

"Good. I return now to the western coast. We will meet at Isca on the fortnight."

" I will be there," Uther said.

Merlin left the hill fort of the Pendragon, and traveled to the west. With each day, hope grew stronger in his heart. Did not the Pendragon seek only what already was in the heart of every Briton...a nation forged of many tribes, capable of ending the Saxon threat for all time, one that would bring peace and prosperity to the island? A great nation for a great land?

For hundreds of years the island had been under Roman rule; now they were themselves defeated. Who would lead the new nation? Ambrosius? No, he did not hold the vision. Uther? Could he understand the needs of the many tribes? Or was there another, still greater, who would come in power to unite the hearts of all peoples of the unborn nation? To fulfill the vision, forge it anew, kindling its flame in every soul?

Ahead, the hills were growing dark. He turned his horse from the road, and dismounted. The rising half moon shined through an opening in the clouds. It was time to meditate on the days ahead. He began to walk into the forest.

Under the trees now, he could barely see his feet beneath him. He walked in slow rocking steps. Something was coming, struggling inside him, an understanding that

would carry him beyond all doubt, into a greater vision of his life and work ahead. But not yet. He was still alone.

Scattered puddles at his feet reflected the light above that filtered through the branches. He used them as a guide to walk the ground.

The sun had not yet left the sky, but lay buried beneath layers of dark gray clouds on the horizon. The land rose slowly upward; the forest thinned. He followed the long gentle slope until he reached the edge of an immense grass-covered plain. A break in the clouds let in a few warming rays from the sun. He listened. There was no sound but the wind traveling lightly over the tall grass. Even the birds were silent.

He had returned to Camulodunum. He walked out toward the center of the plain, almost two miles, deep into the sea of green. No sound.

The power rose up through his body. Understanding came. Here, this would be the place. Here, on a hill within a circle of hills, where sometimes the distant green would be paled by a light mist, as in a dream, sometimes aglow in silver orange, as at twilight. This would be the doorway of the vision. Yes, King Ambrosius and King Uther, I will bring you a giant's dance. I will bring you a place of hope for the gathering of the tribes. I will bring you a united kingdom!

The wind had been rising, growing steadily. The mists were lowering, the breaks in the clouds closing. The air churned; the sky lit up in fire, in explosions that struck the ground in harsh brilliance, blows resounding across the plains. The rain was soft. It wet his eyelashes and ran down his cheeks. He stayed long after his cloak was clinging wet on his skin, standing under the thick clouds, the dark sky, and a few low stars.

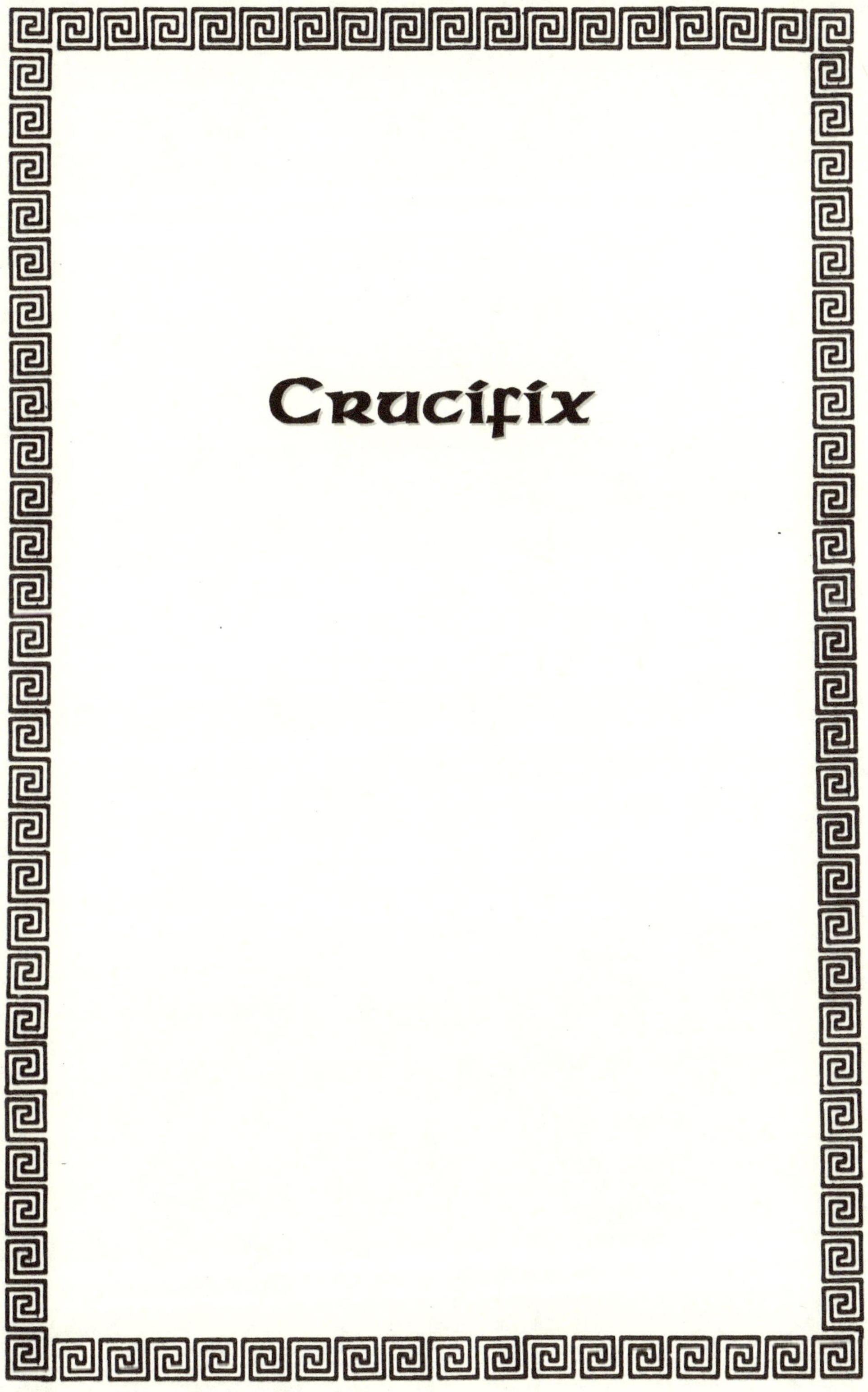

Crucifix

They met at Isca, north of Tintagel by the sea. Uther came in a small swift sailing vessel, flying a sail of midnight blue. With him came sixty of his finest warriors. Merlin was given quarters below, but spent most of his time on deck in the salt air.

They sailed for Tintagel. Long before, Merlin had anticipated his return to this sacred land. Now all was readied for the enactment of the final battle...

In the further meetings of the Amesbury council, Uther had grown bolder in the demonstration of his love. Assured of Merlin's support he no longer attempted to conceal his attraction toward Ygerne. It soon became the private talk of the council members, and made for dissension and uneasiness at the council table. The hope of uniting the clans gave way to fear and mistrust among the would-be allies. The nobles broke again into their original factions. A few appealed to Uther, asking that he cease in his attentions toward Ygerne, for the sake of unity, and for the welfare of the tribes facing the imminent Saxon siege, but he would hear no arguments. Tempers flared.

King Gorlois chose the only course of action open to him. He withdrew from the council along with many of the western nobles, that very night making forced march to his homeland. He knew the wrath of King Uther would soon arise, and his departure would not go unchallenged. Uther had made clear his intent: he would have Ygerne, at whatever cost.

Gorlois rode to Tintagel, the natural fortification of his land. He dispersed the Celtic priesthood and left Ygerne there with a handful of defenders, and then massed his army to the south and east. It had been said of Tintagel that a dozen good knights could hold it against all the armies of the Roman island; it could not be stormed.

As his first hours on the ship passed, Merlin thought of Uther, this man of his own blood. At their first meeting it seemed there was little he could share with him, but now he felt some vague companionship with him, but now he felt some vague companionship growing between them, even if was only that they were soon to risk their lives together...and perhaps there was something more as well. They had both come from diverse ways to heed the one calling of the time. It was true, Uther did not understand the greater meaning of their venture, but he had indeed heard the calling – that was enough.

That first evening of their voyage, he had words with Uther, as they stood at the deck rail looking over the sea.

"There are some things I must speak to you about, Uther. I do not want you to imagine that the success of our venture will be assured by some magical art. There are no protections, only your fate, and mine." Merlin passed before speaking further, carefully considering his next words, "You are neither the first nor the last man who will come to me that I may exercise my power on his behalf. But I tell you now, it does not come at my beckoning or anyone else's – it is only when spirit calls me to do its bidding that I am a giant who no man may stand before."

Uther listened, and was silent for a time. "I fear these things surpass my understanding, but tell me, how fares our undertaking in this light?"

"I have listened to the winds. They have not yet spoken clearly, but I sense our work will be done."

"It is given then?" Uther asked.

"No, nothing is given, only lesser and greater possibilities; we make the pathways," Merlin spoke.

Merlin listened to his own words, and for the first time since his journey had begun long ago, he felt fear, not of

death, but of life. However true and lighted the spirit that had brought him to this moment, it could accompany him nor further.

"You are a strange man, Merlin," King Uther said, but with respect.

They were watching the waves move toward the coastline. Merlin turned to face Uther squarely, and for a moment theirs eyes met, and something was spoken, something more than words could convey. They nodded to one another, knowing their fates were bound together, somehow guided by another hand.

"I have thought unfairly of you, Uther, because it seems you have chosen a path of worldly power. But now I see the accomplishments of this world, too, come forth at the inspiration of the heavens. And one can not always know which realm one traverses," Merlin spoke boldly and truthfully, not sure how Uther might respond.

"May the gods be with us through whatever worlds we must travel," King Uther said.

"Good night, Uther," Merlin said as he departed.

Merlin returned to his cabin below deck.

One there, he sat on his bunk, feeling the pitching of the ship with each wave, and listening to the hard splashing against the wooden hull.

As I approach this first endeavor of worldly partaking, I go alone to my destiny; no human love can offer me strength. But I can hear Ioin's words again...`When there comes to you that unsettling that allows no peace, in a quiet place within your mind, in a windless place within your heart, light a candle. Let its steady flame burn amidst the outer darkness. Know that no eternal sorrow, no unheard asking, no raging turmoil could ever move it to flickering. Return to your first and greatest home. You are that flame.'

But let me sleep now. The coming trial can brook no weariness.

Through the night the ship sailed the coastline, following its jagged path to the south. The winds were steady; by twilight of the next day, they had reached the last spur of land that separated them from Tintagel Head. They dropped anchor.

Merlin was on deck, observing the signs of cloud and the weather. The sky turned black and filled with stars, and thick crescent moon hung low over the horizon. From the west, a bank of gray clouds was slowly approaching.

Merlin turned to Uther and pointed to the clouds. "They are our only hope. This love of yours calls for the dark of a starless night."

So they waited, long into the evening. The small boat was prepared. The clouds had crossed half the sky.

"How much longer, Merlin?" Uther grew anxious.

Merlin looked once more at the cloud cover. "We may go at midnight. But the clouds are still scattered, and may yet prove our undoing. Do you want to go on?"

"My life depends on it," king Uther said.

"And mine," Merlin intoned to himself.

At midnight, they climbed into the small boat. The wind was gusting, and the boat banged against the hull of the ship as it was lowered.

Merlin and Uther each took an oar and pushed off, heading toward the open sea. They rounded the last spur of land.

There it stood, a great towering island of rock, where the earth displayed its belly in walls of gray stone hundreds of feet high, unmoved through centuries of the ocean's fury.

So this would be the womb of Britain, where Uther would lie between Ygerne's parted legs, and conceive the child of a new nation.

He pulled harder against his oar.

"What direction, Merlin?" Uther commanded.

"The northwest corner, where the cliff faces meet," Merlin answered.

The sky was nearly covered in veils of gray clouds, parting occasionally in the wind. When it appeared, the light of the moon was bright, but mostly it remained behind the clouds. The cliffs loomed above them, seeming to rise higher as they approached.

"Quietly on the oars now," Merlin warned, "the sea is calm tonight."

They drew up to the cliffs, near a waist-high ledge. Merlin lifted himself on to it, then jammed the tie rope into a crevice.

"Come on."

Uther pulled himself up.

"Hold your body close to the rock." He stood with his back against the stone, then began to edge his way around the rock wall to the south, balancing himself with hands pressing on the cold stone. He climbed until he was a hundred feet above the waves that crashed on the rocks below, and then waited for Uther. The wind pulled at him.

Above, Ygerne spoke with her guard. "Gawain, my love comes to me this evening by the southern gate. He does not want to be seen by his men, lest they question his leaving of the battle site. Do not detain or question him. Tell Girvin as well. And take your posts ten yards to the south."

"Your grace, Gorlois has said we are to be at your doorway."

"I am your Queen. You have heard my command."

"Yes, your grace," Gawain answered.

On the cliffs, Merlin and Uther had reached a stairway cut into the solid rock. They followed its long ascent to the slopes reaching up to the plateau above,

where Ygerne's cottage lay but a few hundred yards away. On the rim of the plateau, four guards patrolled its perimeter. Merlin and Uther fell flat into the deep wet grass, and waited for them to pass.

"This way, Uther," Merlin whispered.

He led Uther to a stone lined tunnel, a discovery of his earlier wanderings on the island.

"Keep crouched low; the roof will not allow you to stand the entire way. The tunnel ends at a small stone doorway that pulls inward. You then will be only sixty yards from Ygerne, but across open ground. Remember, she has told only her own men. The King's guards would look into anything out of the ordinary, no matter what the explanation. You must not be seen by them. Wait three minutes at the tunnel door after you hear them pass. Only then does the patrol drop slightly below the rim of the plateau. For one minute, perhaps two, you will be out of the range of their vision."

Uther turned to Merlin, and nodded his head in thanks.

"And remember also, when the moon rises above the chapel cross – you can still see its light through these clouds – you must leave immediately or all is lost and we are surely dead. In time of war, the King's own messengers report every two hours, and they will not be deceived."

Uther nodded again, and disappeared into the tunnel. Merlin looked at the low ceiling of misty cloud broken now in patches of dim starlight, and occasional glimmerings of the moon.

Uther groped his way up through the dark tunnel. At the other end, a guard noticed the stone doorway for the first time.

In the dark stillness, Uther felt his life. Memories of his days returned to him. What has led me to this moment, that I would sacrifice all for a woman?

But this is no wild lust, or flush of first love. This possession seems greater than –

The guard pushed open the door. Uther flattened himself against the wall. The glimmer of night light reached into the tunnel, turning the black gray. The tunnel floor was moist and shining. The guard stepped into the low entrance, squatted down, and listened. Uther put his hand on his dagger, and held his breath.

"Reece, bring a torch," said a voice.

Ygerne, alone now in her cottage, grew in fear and doubt. What is this thing that I have begun? Who is this man who now comes to share my marriage bed? The vows of this life are soon forsaken, and my own worthiness soon forsakes me as well, if there be no life after where a heart faithful to greater things is forgiven all transgression. I love him, but I do not yet feel the joy of this approaching union. Perhaps when he is close to me, when I have known him...

Reece came running with a torch, but stopped before he reached the tunnel. "That! You had me leave my post for that old tunnel! Come on, before we both forfeit our heads for your curiosity."

"Alright, then," said the watchful guard, joining his companion. Uther let out a deep breath. He crept toward the doorway. The air was clear again after the dank odors of the tunnel. He listened.

The footsteps of the guards were growing softer.

He began counting to himself to mark the time.

He moved into the night. The guards were not in sight from where he stood.

A trail of about sixty yards led up a gentle slope to Ygerne's cottage. He began to walk in the long stride that would appear to be the King's, drawing his hood down over his forehead, and holding a dagger ready beneath his cloak.

Behind a thinning veil of clouds, the moon shined. more brightly. It crossed into the open sky, casting faint shadows

Thirty more yards. Ygerne's guards had spotted him. Twenty more yards. The moon passed again behind the clouds. Ten more yards. The features of his face were now almost visible to them. He held his head lower and quickened his pace. He would pass directly before them.

He feigned a cough, covering the lower part of his face with his hand Now Ygerne, in perfect grace, took several long slow strides from her doorway, gliding her arm in an outstretched arc to offer her hand to Uther. She swirled, and led him into the hut as the guards watched on, and nodded to one another.

Down on the slopes, Merlin had leaned himself back against a large boulder, just below the perimeter. He drew in a deep breath, and listened, beholding the moment. Above, gulls circling against gray clouds moving over gray sky, far below, the sound of waves climbing rock, exploding upward, pouring back, issuing from the mouths of caves. To the south, a slender sweeping curl of coastland fading into the mist. To the north, a great spur of rock hundreds of feet high set against the sea, sharp cut cliffs, layer upon layer of black rock in crude crystal, a huge arched cave at its base. Beyond, another bay, another spur of coastal rock, a humped-back island at its feet, and then another spur, distant, dark and cut in shadow, a small pointed island at its feet, and another spur, many miles distant, just a dim outline through the mist, and all around, the rippled sea, light and dark seas within seas. And on this rock, his own moonlit shadow, his thoughts, and the first hour passed.

Is this the night I have been brought to, servant to another man's lust? This lone monument of rock God

must have made for this one purpose. In the years to come, it will see the shadow of many a man's passing, but my voice will become as hollow and unknown as the wind over the sea, while this rock will have its claim to eternity from the seed it gives forth...as history's bloody pages spare no words on works of love. For all myself I give to this coming child, but a father of no earthly conception, nor one known of men who see all things physical.

Around him great plates of white rock leaned angled into the ground, rising outward over steep falling earth long hanging sheets of grass touching shelves of rock a hundred feet below, and the rock falling deeper into the ocean cliffs that reached still further down into the depths of the sea. Waiting, the end of the second hour drew near. The wind had grown strong; it whistled over the cliff faces. In only moments it swept the sky of clouds. The moon and stars illuminated the island in a dull yellow haze. Above, the guards were making their round of the perimeter.

"I will walk the slopes one time around," he heard one say, "where the tidings of the sea are better heard." Footsteps broke off from the main group, began descending. Merlin pushed himself deeper into the hollow of the rock. He turned his every sense to the approach. How low would he come? The steps continued to descend, then stopped, about a hundred yards away. For a long time there was no sound. Then they began again, coming across the slope, drawing near.

At the doorway of the cottage, Uther and Ygerne held one another in their arms, for a long moment, touching.

"Come quickly, Uther," Merlin whispered to himself.

Uther kissed her, and began to walk quickly down the pathway.

The moon cleared the chapel cross.

The guard approached. He rounded the last cluster of rock separating himself and Merlin...

"Merlin!?" said the voice as Merlin plunged a dagger deep into his chest. The guard fell forward onto him, down onto his knees, his arms around Merlin's waist.

He turned his face upward. Brennan! His eyes and mouth tried to shout out, `why?' But he was dead. Merlin watched the light leave his eyes, and felt the warm blood running down his own legs. There grew a gaping wound in his own chest, and a sickness in his throat. The sky was drawn as a dark gray sea with islands of black, and the wind carried a light rain; the moon slipped behind a stray cloud, its dim light diffused in but a few shades, the soft whiteness of the rock faces, the waves in blue darkness, the brown earth. The finest mist in a softening veil over all, and the ocean quiet, stirring the night of hidden stars.

He held the red blade before his eyes. It had a dull burnish in the moonlight. He lifted Brennan in his arms, and walked slowly down the slope of grass to the high cliff. He dropped him into the sea. He was left standing motionless, his face lifted into the rain and ocean wind, holding fast to the future, his only hope.

Uther came running down the slope, and seeing the bloody knife in his hand, grabbed it from him and threw it over the cliff. He grabbed Merlin's arm. "Come on." He rushed down the stone staircase, still holding Merlin to his side, carrying him on when he stumbled. And on the cliffs, as they descended, Uther goaded him on, remained beside him, shouting, urging him to fight the battering wind, to not let his will weaken, to not release himself into the peace that beckoned from the jagged rocks far below. They reached the boat, boarded it. Uther put an oar in his hands. He rowed, on and on, as

the steady sea wind dried the dark blood covering his hands.

They met Uther's ship, and sailed until morning, where on the northern coast, they disembarked. Uther offered him a horse for his journey. He refused it.

"Fair journey, prince, your reward will come," Uther called as he rode off with his troop, and Merlin's reply was lost beneath the hoof beats.

"Reward..." Merlin uttered.

He walked alone to the north. Around him, the gray tiny pools of water all around in basins of rock, glimmers of dawn light on the billowing clouds on a background of white streaked blue, a luminous ceiling, the cragged hills like islands in the dimming fog, the circular pouring of the sun's rays through holes in the clouds, on the green sea, rows of white-crested ridges falling one after another onto brown boulders, the coastline fading in either direction, the rush of wind and waves filling the air, no other sound, and the salt spray, and the blowing sand.

The blood on his sleeve grew cold against his skin. He pushed his way inland through crooked branches and thorny ground vines.

He wandered for many weeks through the coastal forests, and then inland. He lost all sense of time and season. Direction, too, left him. But somehow, as though guided by his desire alone, he found her.

As the stars began to fade from the sky, he knelt down beside her, scraping his hand lightly over the soil, and hung his head low.

"Branwen, I have come back to you...for a moment, before I depart, to a place apart from life, a realm not of my making but one that seems for me alone. My journey has been long, and I have learned many things. And I have killed, Branwen, and many of our questions have been answered, but not how we might have hoped." He lifted his head for a moment into the wet wind.

Then he laid his face down on the cold ground, and laid his palms over her resting place.

"But nothing, nothing, nothing seems alive, and nothing is here to touch. Branwen." The wind became a straining whistle, a soft hissing, a murmuring, a hollow echoing.

What is this place of darkness that dreams cannot enter, or day bring justice? What is this silence that is not the peace of evening sleep? What is this emptiness the stars cannot redeem, or love bring serenity?

Looking to the horizon he saw the light before dawn had joined him, lighting the low clouds in hues of rose.

He let it fill him He let it hear him…

Now I know that when I find my place of greatest weakness, there will I find my strength. When I find my place of deepest anger, there will I know my love. And when I find my place of greatest fear, then will my courage never leave me.

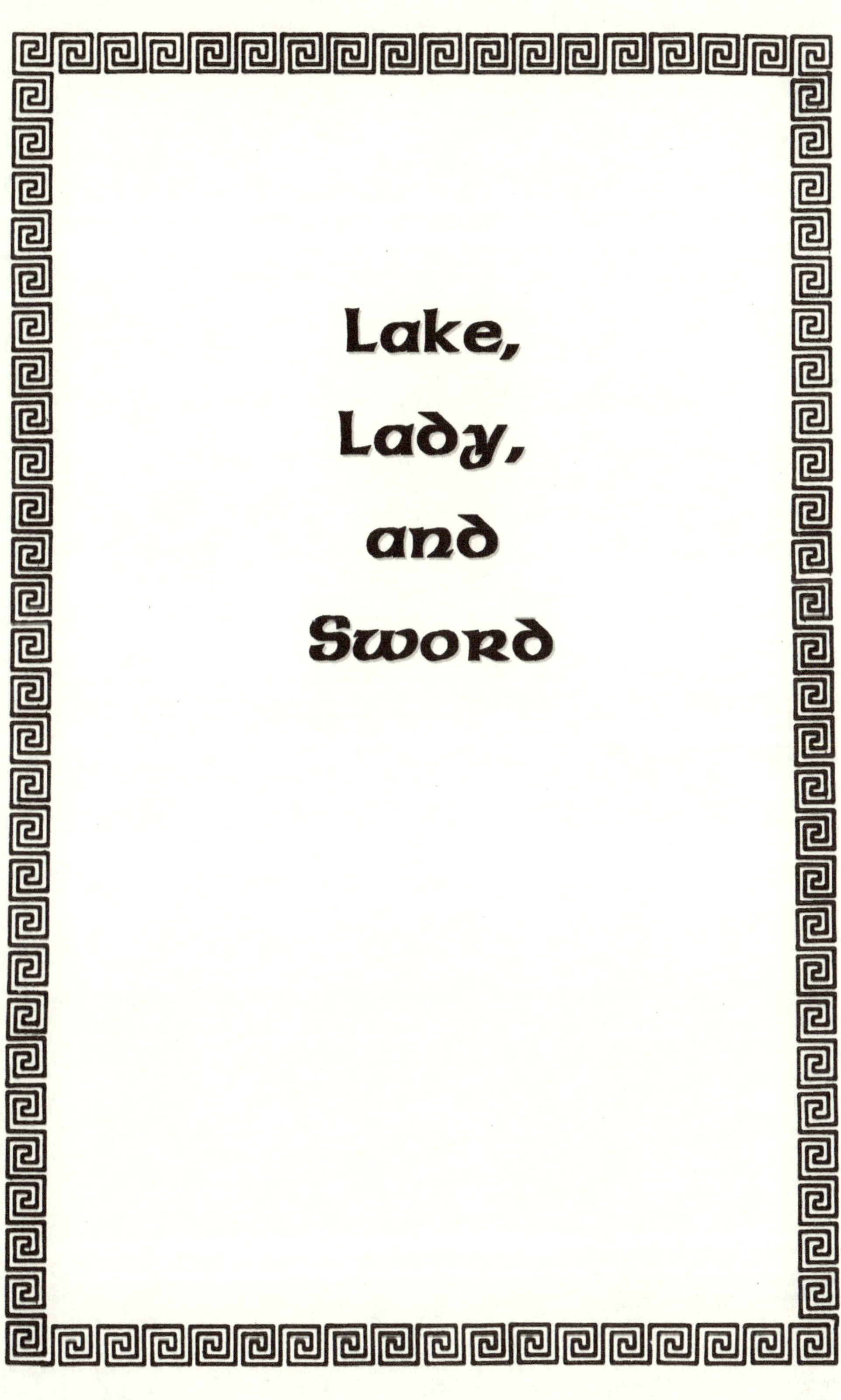

Lake, Lady, and Sword

his morning I awaken unto a darkness that bids I venture forth. But what is there to embrace? I know many weeks have passed, but nothing more. Will this cave no longer hold me? Even this last reminder of substance, this stone that now surrounds me, seems but a veil. Branwen, Ioin, Melchar, you are nowhere to be found; my solitude leaves even memory behind. Only one thing remains – that I have loved you.

At the cave's entrance, fog shifted in the moonlight. He lifted off his blanket, and walked over to the bowl of flame cut into the rock wall. Beside the pool of burning liquid he had once placed three tapers. Now he took one and lit it in the flame. He walked out into the night, his long robe trailing over the ground. The air was cool, damp, lit in moonglow. His feet pressed down onto the layers of rotting gray and brown leaves, the padding of his footsteps the only sound in the valley. He threaded his way down through the slender trees, until he reached the lake's shore, then sat on a large flat stone on the shoreline. He looked over the misty water, over the plain of stillness.

Lady, my gaze falls upon you, trembles, and breaks as a wave upon a tower of rock. I would not dare approach you, lest you dissolve as no more than my own dream. I do not care to know whether you possess substance, or even the most ethereal of form. I will hold you as my perfection, and my fulfillment, my source and my direction.

But let my imperfect words be of no betrayal to you. I know not even my will could bring you forth at a time not of your choosing. And stay beside me now, because I must do what I have sworn to never do again, and if the blood on my hands is cause for God to forsake me, you now will be my refuge, and the mistress I serve, as I go to join my destiny to the life of the one I have begun.

He stood, and walked to the place where his sword lay buried beneath the sand, its grip alone uncovered. He knelt down beside it. He placed his right palm beneath the grip, and began to slowly lift it up, levering it against the point. Stones and sand fell away in a shearing scrape. He unwrapped the oilcloth. The blade shined still, glimmering in the red sun of dawn.

He carried it to the lake. He held it above the water, in the palms of both hands. He lowered it until it was submerged, bathed by the cold water.

And there was a face. Slender lips, a high-ridged nose, dark brown eyes beneath long lashes, black hair. Who knows what I may find within myself when I am alone, truly alone? Bound no longer to things past. What deep fears, what hidden springs of courage? Each movement of the mind is a choosing, each act of love a taking hold.

The senses grasp for what can never truly be held. And how endless is the suffering of seeking, how empty is the desire met. Yet somewhere, I know there is a love not bound by this world of joy and sorrow. For I have learned this: Peace is not an end, nor a fulfillment. It is itself a pathway. Peace is the beginning. Peace is the bounty of ever increasing fire.

He let go his sword, watching it sink to the lake bottom, even as the wind rippled the waters, obscuring it from sight.

The sun now filled the valley with light. His gaze lifted to the green and orange cut block hills. Ancient hills, earned slopes through the ages. Mountains one behind the other, each one higher, a horizon reaching upward toward distant clouds.

Now in his mind and heart rang loud Ioin's words,

"There is another legend, Merlin, concerning this lake. It is said that whoever can find the source of the waters of Llwyn Cerrig Bach will find the ancient Druidic treasures of Anglesey, and the sword of Macsen Wledig."

From the opposite shore, a small river of crystal white climbed rock and grass back into the mountains. He threw his cloak over his robe, and made his way there. He found its meeting place with the lake. He began to walk beside it, following it up through its shallow ravine. Through moss covered rocks, draped green, edges of gray hardness set in soft beds, through a grove of small twisted trees. He would find its source.

The ravine flattened into the hillside. The river parted, became two, became three, became a rushing through the underbrush, a wash over fields of rock, a chiseled gather of clear drapery.

He followed it upward. He bent over to touch a minute princess pine, one of thousands covering the ground all around.

He climbed one mile, and saw the river twisting back into the peaks. His steps now were rhythmic, sure.

He came over a shelf of rock – a cool wind held him, touched his nostrils, mouth, waved over his fingers, lifting his hair.

He looked back.

Brown ridges plunging into lower ridges, into valley.

He walked, saw a lone tree on a rock ledge.

He turned his head in a half circle. One other leafless tree clung to the high cliffs around him. No more for miles.

The fields rock-strewn, grass lying between rocks, more rock than grass. Cut stones washed, rough hewn steps.

He lifted each foot slowly, placed it down.

A few more waves of wind passed over his ears, and the pouring.

Small red berries on the stone slabs.

He reached another ridge, looked back.

The high ridges all around him plunged down into lower ridges, those falling into ridges still lower, sloping down into the valley.

He followed the trail upward. Ledges and peaks falling behind, new ones appearing. The near peaks now seemed no more than a hundred feet above, as the trail led on still higher, towards a last ridge.

The stream silent, its beginnings here. No. Further up, its pouring again.

The ridges – piled blocks, shelves of colored shrubs, red, orange, green

Sky – blue and pale blue, sun in shadow, thin white clouds traveling over. Slopes of sharp cut rock, rock slides.

The ferns blowing, back and forth, back and forth, the ground soggy, compressing under his feet.

Water everywhere through fields and rock beds, around shrubs, ripples, curtains, circles of white foam, lingering in pools, running down. His uncovered feet chilled.

A few breaths.

The highest ridges near, lines of single drops falling from ledges all around, water sheets over laid down grass.

Wind echoing through small caverns of boulders, water pouring from rock, a waterfall of a single current, a hand's width.

The sound of an invisible wind passing underneath rocks. The dripping now only on his right side.

He walked on.

The water deep, far below.

The sound of water gone. But a distant bell tolls.

He cold feel the wind against his ears.

A small trickle down a ledge.

A footstep splashes, flat.

Water at his feet, on the path, running in thin sheets. Steps of stone leading upward. Finger-deep pools shimmering in shadow from gentle current.

Water under rocks, ahead, a new issuing, a new pouring forth.

Two strides ahead, an open stream, water a transparent cross-hatching over flat stones.

To his side, the rhythmic pulse of heavy drops on a ledge.

On every shrub, the closed and faded pink flowers in tiny clusters. A few still rich in color.

A pouring over grass, down small steps, the land at last becoming flat, no longer rising, one last small ridge ahead.

His breath quick, a trace of weariness in his legs.

On his right side still, a ledge of sixty feet.

Tracing its clefts and lines, a small naked tree, a tangle of a few branches holding to the ledge.

The call of a bird, whit-it, whit-it, whit-it.

Flying upward it vanishes into a shrub clinging to the cliff. He was still climbing.

A dry pool of yellow grass amidst all the green.

Sun trying to shine between clouds.

Wind getting colder.

The clatter of loose rocks at his feet.

Ahead, the last small rise of the trail.

Walking in long strides.

The flat land fell away, the ledges parted.

Before him, the open sky.

Far below, a new horizon of low mountains, forests and fields of another valley in colored patches on the hillsides.

A distant expanse of earth marked in sunlight and cloud shadow, through a fine haze.

Wind blowing strong and unrestrained.

On the wall of rock close to him, a crystal stream, only a hand's width, ran down the gray rock.

In one long step he reached it. He leaned over, his palms against the rock face.

Through the curtain of water – he saw it – the glimmering of a sword's steel blade and hilt encrusted with ruby and emeralds. It was the sword.

The sword of Macsen Wledig

He lifted his mouth to the pouring water and drank.

He turned and looked out over the distant horizon, to the blue sky and the high white strands of clouds.

His first journey was ending, another beginning.

There would be a child.

They would build a kingdom.

The water was sweet on his lips.

I alone was to hear these things from Merlin, for great love did he have for me, and I for him, from the moment my mother's handmaiden placed me in his arms on the cliffs of Tintagel.

www.ingramcontent.com/pod-product-compliance
Lightning Source LLC
LaVergne TN
LVHW090937080826
845145LV00003B/789

* 9 7 8 0 9 8 2 4 9 6 8 0 0 *